FitzDuncan's Beginning

John J. Spearman

ISBN: 979-8-9891469-8-7

DEDICATION

This book is dedicated to all the people who have believed
in me, even when it was difficult to do so.

OTHER BOOKS BY THIS AUTHOR

The Halberd Series
Gallantry in Action
In Harm's Way
True Allegiance
Surrender Demand

The Pike Series
Pike's Potential
Pike's Passage
Pike's Progress
Pike's Purpose

The FitzDuncan Series
FitzDuncan
FitzDuncan's Alchemy
FitzDuncan's Enlightenment
FitzDuncan's Fortune
FitzDuncan's Gambit
FitzDuncan's Hope
FitzDuncan's Inheritance
FitzDuncan's Navy

The Perseverance Andrews Series
The Defense of the Commonwealth
The Courage of the Commonwealth
The Resolve of the Commonwealth

The Cliff Rawlins Series
Rawlins' Redemption
SwiftsureAscendant

ACKNOWLEDGMENTS

Many thanks to my editor, Martin Roy Hill, who has been of enormous help
from the standpoints of both technical expertise and moral support.

Deepest gratitude for Thea Magerand, the marvelous artist whose artwork has
brought Caz alive. Every piece she has done for my books amazes me further.

The FitzDuncan books owe a great deal to the inspiration provided by
Alexandre Dumas. Not only do I love his books, the 1973 film version
of *The Three Musketeers* remains one of my favorite all-time movies.

If you would like to stay abreast of my latest activity,
please visit my website: johnjspearmanauthor.com

Foreword

Greetings, dear reader. My name is Robert FitzDuncan Barry Austermain Gau. You probably know me better as Prince Rob. As I mentioned in the last set of scribblings, *FitzDuncan's Peril*, I found some of my father's writings that were never published, and decided to bring them up to date, and included the first grand adventure of my own.

Mr. Gilbert, who unfortunately was killed in the fire in Etiam, had been the driving force in urging my father to write down his tales. His successor as my father's man, Mr. Fields, never knew about this aspect of Mr. Gilbert's service. Without Mr. Gilbert to nag him, my father quit writing after describing the events that took place just before I came into the world.

It's partly my fault, of course. I was born, and they tell me newborns demand a great deal of attention. My mother assures me I was not a difficult baby, but she would say that.

What follows are stories my father wrote down about the period in his life when he first arrived in the capital. I found them in the same drawer as his description of the trip to the southern continent when he and Uncle Fenwick defeated the dark mage in Beata, the capital of Combrial, and then his ill-fated journey north to the Duke of Namie and Baron Westhaver.

As far as I know, these are the only remaining stories my father jotted down. With my father's permission, I decided to finish the job Mr. Gilbert started so long ago. I hope you enjoy them.

1

Spending almost two weeks in a post coach, traveling from the western border to the capital, was a bigger test of my patience than I anticipated. Even worse was the toll it took on my body. Sitting on an uncushioned bench, wedged in with other passengers, in an unsprung carriage, over indifferent roads (or cobblestoned streets when going through towns) was brutal. My back and butt ached in equal portion. Add to that the questionable food served at the inns favored by the operator of the coach service, and I was in rough condition by the time we arrived in Aquileia.

It was raining, of course. When the coach dropped me in the main market square in the city, I needed to pull my oilskin from my pack. First, I needed to wait for the driver to hand it down from above. By the time it was in my hands, I was soaked. My pack was already drenched and heavy, with my few possessions now soggy.

All I had was the name of the inn I should visit—the Foaming Boar. A sergeant who served under me bought it with his retirement payout. Carl Stensland promised me a soft landing when I arrived.

I had never visited the city of Aquileia before, so I had no idea where I was going or even in which direction to start. I asked the driver and he merely gave me a shrug. It was late enough in the day that most shops were closed and the weather was keeping people inside.

Rather than wander aimlessly, I came up with the idea of asking one of the hackney drivers if he knew where it was. The first of three I asked demanded I pay for the information. I understood his need to make some money but thought he was being a bit mercenary. The other two demanded the same.

Finally, I caved in and went back to the first one I asked.

"How much do you want for telling me where I can find the Foaming Boar?"

"A demi-florin," he replied after pondering for a moment.

"How much to take me there?"

"A florin," he said.

"Fine," I said grumpily, acknowledging defeat. "Take me there."

"Coin first, friend," he replied, holding out his hand.

I rolled my eyes and retrieved my money pouch. It was depressingly light and would be until I could get to a bank. Fishing inside, I found a florin and gave it to him.

"Get in, then," he instructed.

The interior of the hackney was at least an improvement over the post coach. For one thing, the seat was upholstered. For another, it had an actual pane of glass for a window, instead of a rolled down piece of canvas, so it was dry.

Even though the carriage had springs, they did not help much with the cobbled pavement. The vibration made my teeth rattle. It was a short ride—less than three minutes. That frustrated me when I realized how close I had been.

He dropped me at the front door. Sure enough, the sign overhead depicted a boar foaming at the mouth in mid-charge. I threw my pack over my shoulder and stepped inside.

It was warm and dry. There was a hum of conversation in the common room from a dozen guests. While I stood dripping on the floor, I looked around to see if I could spot Carl. It made me feel awkward, as he did not appear immediately.

Eventually, he breezed in, carrying two steins in each hand, delivering them to a group of men seated in the common room. When he placed them on the table, someone else caught his attention. He hurried to them with his back to me. It took another minute for him to hear their request before he turned around.

"Cap'n! Be right with you," he called.

He disappeared into the back again. When he emerged, he was carrying two more steins. Carl came to me and handed me one, then gestured to a comfortable-looking chair in the common room near the fireplace.

"Good to see you, Cap'n," he said with a grin as he sat down. "Just mustered out?"

"Aye, Sar'nt. Then twelve days in a post coach, and here I am."

"Well, your troubles are over temporarily," Carl said. "I have a room for you upstairs. Dinner is cooking and will be ready soon—roast fowl tonight. There's more cider where that came from, or ale if you prefer."

"Cider is fine, Sar'nt. I'll just sit here and try to dry out," I said. "Not that it will do much good. Everything I own—"

"Cap'n, I promised I'd take care of you," he said. "Take your drink and go on up to room four. Put all your wet things outside the door. I'll have a girl drop off a shirt and a pair of breeches. She'll take your wet things, and I'll have 'em clean and dry by morning."

"I can't put you to that much trouble, Carl."

"No trouble at all," he grinned. "I'm not going to be the one to wash 'em. I have an arrangement with a laundress around the corner. You're early enough that she can get 'em done by morning. Then, after breakfast tomorrow, we'll draw you a nice hot bath."

"Majors and Minors, Carl! It's been a couple of years since I enjoyed that much luxury," I said.

"I reckoned," he said. "Don't worry about anything, Cap'n. We'll get you on your feet solid here in Aquileia."

The dinner that evening was immensely superior to anything I ate at the inns the post coach used. As promised, my clothes—the few I had—were clean and dry in the morning. Then, after breakfast, I was treated to my first hot bath in over a year.

"That's a big improvement over the drowned rat who arrived last night," Carl said when I appeared in the common room.

"Thank you, Sar'nt," I replied. "I feel almost human again."

"So, Cap'n, what will you do now that you're mustered out?"

"I don't really know, Carl. And seeing how we're both no longer Rangers, you can call me Caz."

"I'll try, but some habits are hard to break," Carl said. "If you don't mind me asking, how are you fixed for funds?"

"I'm comfortable enough," I replied.

In truth, between a small inheritance from my grandfather, my mustering out money, and my accumulated pay as a Ranger (which I rarely spent), I had over two thousand ducats in the bank. When my grandfather died, he left me a small bequest that was paid out at a hundred ducats a year. With it and my savings, I could afford to buy a small plot of land and live comfortably, but the prospect bored me.

I spent seven years in the Rangers, rising to the rank of captain on my own merits. The next rank, major, required one of two things—ten thousand ducats to purchase a commission, or a friend at the court. I realized I possessed neither.

Prince Albert and Prince Wim both served in the Rangers with me, but I was not close to either. Albert was an arrogant prig. Wim was more approachable, but we did not have a close enough friendship for me to ask for that large of a favor.

I decided my time in the Rangers was over. Without any idea of what I planned to do to make a living, I headed to the capital, Aquileia. Now that I was here, I hoped something might present itself. In the meantime, I had enough money to enjoy myself for a few years as long as I did not indulge in extravagance.

"The reason I ask, Cap'n, is that those clothes just won't do," Carl said. "You're a respectable man. Except for your jacket, those clothes make you look like you just rode in from the farm—and not a very successful one at that. Other than your Rangers jacket, which you shouldn't wear anymore, about the only thing that's decent is your boots. In order to get you off to a good start here in the city, you need to present a more reputable appearance."

"Carl, I've worn the uniform for seven years," I explained. "These clothes date back to when I joined up. They are all I have."

"Well, you need better," Carl stated in a no-nonsense tone. "Go see Hamed Erdogan, the tailor. He'll get you sorted out properly and won't hurt your purse … much."

I set out midmorning. The first stop was the bank. My account was with Farmer & Mercantile. The only reason is they were the institution that managed the annuity from the grandfather.

For those of you who are new to my tales, I suppose I ought to tell you a bit more about me. I'm a bastard, you see. Not in terms of morals and behavior, mind you—I was raised a gentleman and strive to conduct myself as one. No, my birth was illegitimate. My father, Duncan Barry, is Earl of the Eastern March. My mother was one of the housemaids, and quite pretty, from what I was told. He was unmarried at the time of the dalliance.

Due to my illegitimate birth, I was not allowed to use the surname Barry. Instead, my surname is FitzDuncan. In the country of Aquileia, that denotes that I am the bastard son of someone named Duncan.

When I was three years old, my father married a woman from the city of Aquileia named Veronica. My grandfather sent my mother away, and set her up as a seamstress in a country town far away. I remained at Easton Manor.

My stepmother would barely tolerate my presence when either my father or grandfather were nearby. When they were absent, she would curse me and cuff me if I strayed too close. My father began spending more and more time away, tending to the needs of the March. My grandfather took over raising me.

When I was thirteen, Veronica gave birth to a son—Edwin. My grandfather decided it was best if I left home—permanently, as it turned out. I went away to boarding school. The only time I was allowed to return to Easton was for his funeral, less than three years later. I was not permitted to stay in the manor—I had a room at one of the inns in Easton. By then, Veronica had produced another son, Percival.

When he died, my grandfather left me the annuity I've mentioned, as well as his sword. Of the two, I value the sword more. It's a beautiful weapon—a rapier with a blade of nine parts and a swept hilt. The blade is, of course, a single piece. The nine parts refer to the different composition of the steel with which each section is made. Marvelously balanced, it is stiff at the hilt and gradually more flexible at the tip. Looking at it, you can't tell where one section ends and the next begins.

Upon receiving this gift, I devoted myself to the study of fencing. I felt a responsibility to train myself to be worthy of such a fine weapon. By the time I left the place, the only person at school who would spar with me was the fencing master. My schoolmates wearied of losing to me.

When my time at school ended, I joined the Rangers as a cadet. The Rangers patrol our western border, engaging in regular skirmishes with our age-old enemies, the Rhetians. Life in the Rangers suited me well. Within a year, I was promoted to lieutenant. Two years later, I was named a captain.

In the Rangers, I learned that fencing was only a part of fighting. Fisticuffs and wrestling were also important if you wanted to stay alive. I knew nothing about those when I joined. Thank all the heavenly beings, I learned quickly. Carl actually tutored me in wrestling for a time.

It took a bit of time for me to convince the people at Farmer & Mercantile that I was indeed, Casimir FitzDuncan. They were having difficulty believing that someone attired as I was could hold an account with over two thousand ducats. Eventually the man in charge decided my mustering-out papers were good enough to prove my identity. I left with a hundred ducats in my now heavy purse.

Hamed Erdogan took one look at me and wrinkled his nose. His expression improved when I told him I knew I needed an entire wardrobe. He set to measuring.

"What exactly are you looking for, Mr. FitzDuncan?" he asked.

"Respectability, I suppose," I answered. "I don't want to look like a tradesman, but I would like my clothes to be nearly as sturdy. Even though I was raised as a member of the gentry, I prefer my mode of dress to be simpler and more practical than fashionable."

"I believe I know exactly what you seek," Erdogan said. "The Duke of Manton is a customer. He is not afraid to get his hands dirty when he is at home. His clothing needs to be, as you said, sturdy."

Hearing that Erdogan counted the duke among his customers cheered me. His son, Lord Rawlinsford, was a classmate and one of the few friends I had at school. Freddy, the name I knew him by, was one of only three schoolmates who invited me to come home with them. The rest of the time, I spent school breaks as the only student on the grounds.

"I know the duke," I said, "and if you can have me looking like him without draining my purse, I'll be a happy customer."

Hamed and I agreed on four pairs of breeches, eight shirts, a cravat of middling quality and subdued pattern, two waistcoats, some underclothes and stockings, and a jacket. Given that it was still spring, I also bought an oilskin to protect me from the rain.

"Hamed, I have one unusual request regarding the jacket," I said.

"What sort of request?"

"I need you to alter the hem," I said. "Please sew a row of demi-florins inside the jacket from end to end, along the edge."

Hamed gave me a puzzled look.

"I wish to add weight to the hem," I explained. "If I find it necessary to defend myself, being able to use my jacket as a sort of weapon might save my life."

"Do you expect to be in that much danger?" Erdogan asked.

"I have no idea," I confessed. "Until recently, I was in the Rangers on the western border. This is my first visit to the capital. I certainly hope I am not attacked, and don't plan to seek any confrontations, but one never knows when trouble will occur in the city."

Erdogan nodded and began tallying the cost of my purchases. I looked as he added the figures. The total came to just under forty ducats.

"Mr. Erdogan," I said before he shared the number with me, "I will confess I am not worldly wise. May I ask if this is a firm number, or am I expected to haggle with you?"

"I like you, Mr. FitzDuncan," he said with a chuckle. "Honesty like that is refreshing. I would expect to argue over the price."

"If that is something you enjoy, I don't wish to disappoint you," I said. "What sort of counter-offer would a more experienced man suggest?"

"One of my regular customers would begin to mention how poorly his business was doing this year, or how thin the crops came in last fall, and tell me that he regretted that he could only offer me thirty ducats at most."

"In my case, I just left the Rangers and have not yet found a new source of income, so must exist entirely on my meager savings," I said.

"Perfect," Erdogan commented. "Then I would discuss how my three children were growing like weeds, and eating far more than any human should be able to. I would also add that the cost of their schooling is a heavy burden, and that I could not possibly do this amount of work for less than thirty-eight ducats."

"Would I then refer to my horse's recent case of colic, and suggest thirty-two ducats would be the absolute most I could spend?" I asked.

"And I would share with you that my wife's family was planning on moving to the city and living with us, and I could not settle for less than thirty-six ducats," Erdogan stated with a grin.

"I'm having trouble thinking of a convincing lie," I admitted. "Would we eventually settle on thirty-five ducats as a fair and reasonable price for this work?"

"We would."

"Here are thirty-five ducats, Mr. Erdogan," I said. "I apologize for not being better prepared for this part of the transaction. In the fall, I will need winter clothing, and I promise to hold my end of things up much better."

On my way back to the Foaming Boar, I passed a bookseller's shop. There was a sign in the window indicating rooms for rent. I went inside. The man who I presumed was the owner was standing in the back. He gave me a skeptical look.

"Are you Mr. Forteney?" I asked.

"Who wants to know?"

"My name is Casimir FitzDuncan," I said. "I saw the sign in the window. Please don't be put off by the appearance of my clothes. I just mustered out of the Rangers and have no regular clothes yet. I just visited a tailor and should present a more reputable appearance in a few days."

"Which tailor?"

"Hamed Erdogan."

"Is there anyone nearby who will vouch for you?"

"Carl Stensland," I said. "The owner of—"

"I know Carl. Yes, I'm Lyle Forteney," he said, offering his hand. "Are you only visiting the city, or planning on living here?"

"Living here," I said.

"Let's go upstairs, then. I'll show you the rooms."

2

We went up a staircase at the rear of the shop. Forteney explained there was also a separate entrance on the side of the building. The door opened to a flight of stairs leading to a door off the small kitchen of the flat.

In addition to the kitchen, there was a decent-sized sitting room with a fireplace and a bedroom. There wasn't a stick of furniture in the place, but the kitchen contained some pots and pans, plus place settings for four. There was also a tin bathtub and a couple of buckets tucked away in the tiny pantry.

Even though a noticeable layer of dust coated everything, it looked to be just about perfect for me. The building was on a market square in a respectable part of the city. I would not be embarrassed by my address.

"How much are you asking for it?" I inquired.

"Two ducats a month," Forteney replied.

"That explains the layer of dust on everything," I commented. "You've been trying to let these rooms for a few months, then. How about one ducat, twelve florins?"

"Two ducats a month and a hot bath once a week," Forteney countered with a grin, warming to the idea of bargaining.

"One ducat, twelve florins," I repeated, "with the hot bath added because with me living above the shop, you can rest easy at night and not worry about burglars."

"One ducat, twenty florins, with the weekly bath, plus wood for the stove or the hearth," he said.

"One ducat, sixteen florins for all that, paid six months in advance," I countered.

One ducat, eighteen florins, and I have a woman named Placida come and clean the rooms every week and do your laundry, paid a year in advance," Forteney said.

"Done, if you have the place swept out in the next day," I said and offered my hand.

"Done," he agreed as we shook.

I pulled twenty-one ducats from my now lighter purse and handed them to Forteney. He took them and gestured to the stairs. I followed him down into the book shop. He went behind a desk and began writing out a receipt.

"When you're finished with that, Mr. Forteney, would you also please jot down the terms we just agreed to?" I asked.

"Do you want a contract?" he asked.

"I don't think we need that degree of formality," I said. "I just don't want there to be any reason we should argue between now and next year."

After he finished the receipt, Forteney wrote down the terms to which we agreed on two sheets of paper. We initialed both copies. He slid his into the desk.

I returned to the inn. The lunch crowd was gathering. It was made up mostly of shopkeepers from nearby. When the crowd thinned out, Carl stopped by.

"I've ordered some clothes," I said. "Erdogan's prices seemed reasonable. I've also rented rooms."

"Really? Where?"

"Above a bookseller."

"I was going to suggest you speak with Lyle," Carl said. "You'll need furniture."

"I will. You've seen the rooms, I take it?"

"I did—a couple of months back," Carl said. "I was surprised no one took them before now."

"He wanted two ducats a month," I said.

"That explains why they were still empty. I hope you're not paying that much."

"It's a little on the high side," he said after I shared the end result of my negotiations with him. "Having the woman come to clean and do your washing probably makes up for it, though."

"Where can I find furniture?" I asked.

"I know a man," Carl said. "You'll need to take him to the rooms. I imagine you'll want a sofa, and he will need to build it in place. There would be no way to get it up the stairs otherwise. The other pieces should be no problem—table, chairs, a couple of comfortable armchairs, and a bed. You'll want a couple of rugs, too. I have the name of someone who can make them for you."

After showing the rooms to the carpenter who specialized in making furniture, and ordering two rugs—one for the sitting room and another for the bedroom—most of the hundred ducats I withdrew from the bank that morning was spent. It was by far the most expensive day of my life up to that point. Still, I knew that it would be, and was slightly smug that I guessed a hundred ducats would be enough to accomplish what I did.

A week later, I collected my new clothes from Hamed, left the inn, and moved into my new rooms. After putting my things away, I sat down in my newly constructed armchair. I imagined the king must feel the way I did, when he sits on the throne. Now all I needed was a way to make a living.

I'd spent a good portion of the previous week wandering through the city, hoping I might find some inspiration. Two things became apparent. One was that I possessed nothing in the way of a marketable skill. The other was that I did not want to deal with the general public.

I was good with a blade and a bow, and an excellent rider, but there wasn't much call for that in the city. Looking at people like Hamed Erdogan and Lyle Forteney, I did not possess the temperament to deal with customers all day, every day. I would not classify myself as a loner, but I was quite independent. The number of people I considered friends could be counted on both hands with fingers left over.

Much of that had to do with the circumstances of my birth. Growing up in Easton, I was not allowed to play with the children in the city, because my father was Lord Easton. My companions were the armsmen employed to defend the March from the annual visits of the horse nomads who arrived from the east every summer and stayed through the late fall. Then my grandfather sent me away when my half-brother was born.

At school, my fellow students were members of the nobility (and even the royal family) or the sons of wealthy traders and merchants. I was the target for abuse of all kinds. Only a few people—three, in fact—looked beyond my bastardy to see what sort of person I was.

After school, I joined the Rangers and was quickly put in a position of command. As a result, I kept my own counsel. I depended on no one. In fact, for the last seven years I have been more used to people depending on me.

In my wanderings the next day, I found a salle d'armes. Since I was no longer in the Rangers, I no longer had the opportunity to train regularly. A salle was a place to continue that training.

That evening, I found myself outside an inn named the Brass Frog at dinner time. I heard it was one of the better inns in the city, so decided to give it a try. A very pretty girl with blue eyes and black hair showed me to a small table in the corner of the dining room. Her dress had a low-cut bodice.

At the time, I thought she was behaving oddly. She fluttered her eyes at me and touched me with her hand more often than I thought was necessary. When I sat down, she bent over in front of me, presenting her damned attractive bosom to my gaze. She told me her name was Jenny, and squeezed my hand as she said it.

You have to remember that, up to this point in my life, I had no experience with women at all—none. I learned later that Jenny was flirting with me—she told me so. At the time, I didn't know what to think.

Shortly after, she brought my dinner—again bending over in front of me. It was a good meal—nothing fancy, but done perfectly When I finished eating, I went to settle with the innkeeper.

I left the inn and headed out on the street, passing a group of four men. My head was down, and I was not paying much attention. Thank all the heavenly beings one of them was.

"Caz?" I heard one of them call out uncertainly.

I turned around. Standing in the group of four were Lord Rawlinsford and Linc Ellsworth. Freddy and Linc were two of the three schoolmates who brought me home with them during school breaks. Upon seeing me, Freddy charged toward me. Linc was not far behind, though more graceful.

"Caz!" Freddy shouted as he enfolded me in a bear hug a step ahead of Linc.

"Hello, Freddy. Hello, Linc," I said, freeing my right arm to clasp Linc's hand.

"What are you doing in the city?" Freddy gushed.

They invited me to join them. Linc introduced me to RJ Sweetland and Paul Fassbender. I told them I left the Rangers, had moved to the city, and was looking for a way of earning of living. None of them offered any ideas.

They had been playing cards all afternoon. Linc and Paul were the winners. The Brass Frog was near to where all of them lived, so they stopped in for dinner, with the winners to pay for the meal.

I entertained them with stories of my time on the border with the Rangers. Freddy and Linc caught me up with what they had been doing since school—not much. Paul Fassbender had a sister, Nellie, who was the object of Linc's affection. RJ Sweetland was originally a friend of a friend. Freddy seemed subdued compared to the gregarious nature I remembered.

We were the last to leave the dining room. Once again, Jenny made eyes at me. Linc noticed it.

"You need to follow up on that, Caz," he said.

"On what?"

"That girl is mighty interested in you, Caz."

"How do you know?"

"Do you think she gives looks like that to everyone?"

"I have no idea."

"Trust me," Linc said, patting me on the shoulder. "I guarantee it will be worth your time."

Linc, RJ, and Paul said their goodnights, but Freddy lingered. He invited me to follow him home for a glass of sherry. I could tell he had something he wanted to discuss.

We walked to his house, only three blocks away. The house actually belonged to his family. Freddy's father was the Duke of Manton, and Freddy would inherit the title when his father passed on.

Freddy led me into the house. His servant Roger was still awake. Freddy asked him to light some candles and then suggested he retire for the evening. When Roger left the room, Freddy poured two glasses of sherry and sprawled out on his sofa.

His posture brought back memories. Freddy never sat up when he could spread out. I waited for him to speak.

"I'm in terrible trouble, Caz," he said with a sigh. "And you might be the perfect person to help me out."

"What sort of trouble?"

"I've lost my ring," he said. "It's a family heirloom. My father is coming to visit in a month, and I need to have it back by then."

"When you say you lost it, is it missing? After all, Aquileia is a big city, and—"

"I lost it in a card game to Sir Edmund Tourville."

"From the tone of your voice and the expression on your face, there is more to the story," I commented. "Why don't you start at the beginning?"

"I belong to the Equestrian Club," Freddy said. "Generally, I ride most mornings, then stop in the club and have lunch. Often there are card games following the meal. I was invited to join a group of men whose fourth was absent. I know two of them from the club. The other man, Tourville, was a guest."

"We played plafond that afternoon," he continued. "Tourville wasn't especially good. He complained that the game was too predictable, and the stakes weren't high enough. His game, he said, was San-Sa. That intrigued me. I hadn't played San-Sa since we were at school together. Compared to Plafond, luck plays a much greater role, and I remember the game being damned exciting when we played—except when you sat in."

I laughed.

"Caz, you were the best San-Sa player of us all," Freddy said. "You never left the table with less money than you brought."

"I remember asking you to hold my winnings, so when the others came to thrash me to get me to give it back, I could honestly say I didn't have it," I said.

"You did take some frightful beatings, Caz," Freddy said, shaking his head. "Anyway, Tourville convinced me to join him that night at an inn, the One-Eyed Cat."

"With a name like that, I expect it was in the Kettle or down by the docks," I said.

"Actually, it's not far," Freddy said. "The food is good. Their sherry is only middling."

"Go on," I suggested.

"I went with Tourville that night, and played with him and four other men in a private dining room. He introduced me, but none of them was particularly memorable. The game was as much fun as I remembered, and I walked away nearly a thousand ducats to the good."

"Majors and Minors!" I gasped.

"Because I was the big winner, all of them prevailed upon me to join them the next night," Freddy continued. "Again, I walked away at the end of the evening several hundred ducats to the good. They begged me to come back to have a chance at regaining their losses. That third night, we played until late. All of us were drinking rather heartily, and the bets for each hand grew larger and larger. I'd not done as well as the previous two nights, and I suppose I was down about four thousand ducats."

"Only half that, though, with your previous winnings," I commented.

"No," Freddy said sadly. "I'd lost what I won the night before and was down four thousand on top of that. Then I got the hand I had been waiting for all night—three and two, kings over queens. Tourville either held a good hand or was bluffing, and stayed in. Finally, he raised. In order to see his cards, I needed three thousand ducats in addition to the three thousand I'd already committed to this hand."

"Majors and Minors, Freddy!" I exclaimed. "Surely you didn't arrive at the inn with a chest of gold. How were you going to settle this debt?"

"With a bank draft, I thought. Tourville asked the same question. He was very polite but asked for some kind of surety that I would return the next day with it in hand."

"Was the ring his idea or yours?" I asked.

"Actually, his, now that you mention it," Freddy said.

"Oh, Freddy," I sighed.

"Caz, I'm not a complete fool," Freddy protested. "I knew I was in trouble. Explaining away ten thousand ducats to my father would be impossible. But I was convinced I held the winning hand. All night long, once I started losing, I looked for evidence of cheating. I didn't see anything, but that doesn't mean it was an honest game."

"You lost the hand," I observed.

"I most certainly did," Freddy said glumly. "We laid our cards down. I put my kings over queens on the felt. Tourville set out four singletons. Tourville was very gracious and said I would be able to find him at the inn around lunchtime the next day."

"Did he disappear? Is that how you lost the ring?" I asked.

"No, he was there when I arrived the next afternoon with my bank draft in hand," Freddy said. "When I gave him the draft, he told me that he had a change of heart. If I wanted the ring back, I needed to give him a hundred thousand ducats."

"Freddy, please don't take offense, but does your family have that kind of money?"

"We do," he said, "but it has been accumulated by the careful management of generations of my forebears. My father is allowing me to live relatively carefree for now because once I take over, he knows it will be nothing but work. He never had the chance to enjoy himself, and wanted me to indulge."

"Is any piece of jewelry worth a hundred thousand ducats?" I asked.

"No," Freddy answered. "it's not even worth the ten thousand Tourville already has. It does have value within the family, though. It has been handed down from eldest son to eldest son for more than ten generations. Losing the ring on top of ten thousand ducats will be more than I think my father will be able to forgive."

"So, how can I help?" I asked.

"I want you to expose Sir Edmund Tourville as a cheat," he said. "I want my ring back, and the ten thousand. You are the best card player I've ever met. If anyone can do it, you can."

3

"Freddy, in order to do this, I'll need to pass myself off as far wealthier than I am," I said. "Plus, I don't have that much I can wager."

"I'll back you," Freddy said. "We'll need to get you some nicer clothes. No offense intended, Caz, but you need to look rich. Right now, you look like my father."

"I used his tailor," I said.

"That would explain it," Freddy said with a smile. "We'll go to mine. I'll also give you three thousand ducats to play with. When this is done, you'll give it back. Anything you make above that, you keep. If you lose all of it, you don't owe me anything."

"Tell me more about what happened at the One-Eyed Cat," I asked. "Were the players the same all three nights?"

"They were."

"That means they are all part of Sir Edmund's scheme," I said. "I assume the deal rotated from player to player?"

"It did."

"And you watched carefully?"

"At first I did since I did not know these men," Freddy said. "When I started winning, I quit paying close attention until the last night when the cards went cold for me."

"Did you see anything suspicious?"

"I did not catch them doing anything," Freddy admitted, "but they were all well-practiced card handlers, if that makes sense."

"Like Tommy Robinson?" I asked, referring to a schoolmate who used to practice sleight-of-hand card tricks.

"Very much like Tommy," Freddy agreed. "Again, I did not catch them, but I certainly suspected something wasn't right."

"You should have left at that point," I commented.

"I know, Caz. I've kicked myself at least a hundred times," he said. "But I drank just enough that my pride got in the way of my common sense."

"Did they use the same deck of cards all night?"

"The last night I asked them to change," Freddy said. "I laughed it off, saying that the deck we were using was obviously unfriendly."

"Did they resist your idea?"

"No."

"They changed the deck while you were there?" I asked.

"Now that you mention it, no. Sir Edmund suggested we take a short break to relieve ourselves. When we returned to the table, a different deck was in play—blue instead of red."

"Did everyone leave the room at the same time?"

"No," Freddy said, shaking his head sadly.

"I must say, Freddy, this sort of recklessness doesn't sound like you," I remarked.

"It's not," he sighed. "I've been bored, though. This was something new. The risk made it more attractive."

"Tell me more about Sir Edmund," I requested. "Where does he come from?"

"Somewhere out west," Freddy said. "North of Dunland, someone said. He's only a baronet, so his holding isn't large. That part of the country isn't known for much."

"The people who invited him to the Equestrian Club—?" I started to ask.

"Do not know him well," Freddy answered quickly. "I'd never heard of him before this, and, well, I know everyone."

"I'm sure you do," I said with a chuckle. "Now, if we're going to pass me off as someone wealthy, who should it be?"

"I already have an idea," Freddy said. "Baron Winstonworth—out east—just died. You could say you are Brantford."

"Freddy—Brantford Winstonworth is a turd," I complained.

"I know," Freddy said with a laugh. "If you happen to sully his name in the process of getting my ring back, it will be a form of justice."

I shook my head in mild disbelief.

"Please, Caz?" Freddy asked.

"Freddy, I'll do my absolute best to help you," I said.

"Thank you, Caz. Let's meet mid-morning at my tailor—say, ten o'clock? We'll get you some new clothes."

Walking back to my rooms above the bookseller, I considered Freddy's problem. I will admit that I was good at cards. I preferred Plafond, but in school, we played San-Sa.

Mostly as a result of my status as a bastard, I learned early in my school days to keep emotions from my face. Showing emotion gave my tormentors leverage. In San-Sa, being able to mask one's feelings was an asset.

I was also good at detecting the tics people displayed upon seeing whether they held good or weak hands. In addition, I learned to spot cheaters. You would think that the sons of the nobility would never stoop so low, but you would be wrong.

With a table full of accomplices, Sir Edmund would have plenty of assistance in mucking and culling cards. Mucking cards meant hiding them, either in your hand or on your person. Culling was the term used to describe arranging the deck to deal desired cards to yourself, your opponent, or a confederate.

What Freddy described that happened to him on the last hand was a typical ploy I first saw used against me at school. The dealer purposely dealt me a good hand. He gave himself a better one. Before things progressed, I noticed from the set of his eyes that he had complete confidence he would win the hand. I folded right away. The look of disappointment on his face was clear.

Almost every time while I was at school, I walked away from the table with the other players' money in my purse. My success, even when my opponents attempted to cheat, infuriated them. It was not unusual for the losers to corner me later and administer a whupping, trying to get me to surrender the money I'd won from them.

At first, I had little choice. Handing over the money would not end the beating, though. They would continue until they were well satisfied. After I made friends with Freddy, Linc, and Ratty Hawkins, I would find a way to pass them my purse secretly before I left the room. I also got better at defending myself—at least, as much as one can against a group of three or four. Though I would end up battered, my assailants would not escape unscathed.

Black eyes, a swollen nose, and fat lips were common facial features for me at school. The faculty seemed not to care. After all, I was a bastard. It was enough that they allowed me to attend in the presence of my "betters."

We met the next day outside Freddy's tailor. He had me fitted for three complete suits of new clothing, all finer than what I recently obtained from Hamed Erdogan. It cost Freddy nearly three hundred ducats.

"It will be money well spent, if it achieves our objective," Freddy said. "If it doesn't, then it's just another foolish decision I've made."

"I know you want to keep this a secret, Freddy, but to pull this off, we need one more person," I said on our way back to his house after the visit to the tailor.

"What do you mean?" he asked.

"If they follow the same plan as before, they'll let me win the first two nights," I explained. "The third night, the cards will turn against me. I'm going to demand that we bring in someone else to deal the cards. If you could arrange for, say, Linc and Ratty and two other people to be playing plafond or something in the common room of the inn, that would be helpful. Each of them should also be carrying a new deck of cards with a different backing than the red or blue ones you used before."

"What are you going to do?"

"I'm going to catch Sir Edmund cheating," I said. "And threaten to expose him unless he returns your ring and bank draft. Under the Code of Honor—"

"I knew there was a reason they made us memorize that stupid thing," Freddy said.

Before the earliest recorded history of Aquileia, judicial courts were few. As a result, men developed rules for settling disputes without the intervention of a formal court. These rules were compiled into the "Code of Honor." As formal courts became more numerous, the purpose of the Code shifted to focus almost exclusively on personal disagreements—matters of honor, in particular—things that could not be resolved in court.

The biggest portion of the Code dealt with offenses to one's personal honor. Dueling was the preferred method of resolving these issues, and all the proper procedures, challenges, and responses were spelled out. Games of chance and wagers were a smaller section of the Code. Gambling debts, for instance, were to be settled within a day in the manner chosen by the winner.

In this respect, Sir Edmund was within his rights to hold Freddy's ring for ransom. He agreed to it as collateral. It now belonged to him. According to the Code, the gambling debt was settled when Sir Edmund agreed to accept the ring. Therefore, even though the amount he was demanding from Freddy was far in excess of the amount of the original wager, the Code did not apply.

Cheating was covered by the Code. A man who cheated at games of chance was considered no gentleman, and should be shunned by every member of "polite society." It would certainly affect Sir Edmund's standing with the royal court, and would probably cost him the territory he was holding in fief.

We were near the Brass Frog by now, and it was midday. I was intrigued by what Linc said about Jenny the night before. Perhaps she was there and I could learn more.

"Let's stop in for lunch," I suggested.

My luck was good. Jenny was indeed there and immediately came to our table. She was polite to Freddy but smiled broadly and batted her eyelashes at me. When she brought us mugs of cider, she bent lower than necessary to serve mine.

"That young lady wants to get to know you much better, Caz," Freddy commented.

"That's what Linc said last night."

"Well, what are you going to do about it?"

"Freddy," I said, dropping my voice to a whisper, "I have no experience with women."

"You're joking."

"I swear on all the heavenly beings, Freddy," I whispered.

"You do *like* girls, don't you?" Freddy asked.

"Yes, and I find Jenny extremely pretty, but I have no earthly idea what to do," I confessed.

"You've never—?"

"Freddy, I went from school to the Rangers," I explained. "I've been on the western border for the last seven years."

"You never went into town, and, uh—"

"No," I said. "The idea of paying a woman—especially of the sort who were available—it didn't interest me much. I don't think I saw more than a handful of young attractive girls in the entire time I was there, and they all seemed quite married."

"Oh, my," Freddy sighed sympathetically. "Well, no time like the present to begin your education."

"What do you mean?"

"Jenny, would you please come here a moment?" Freddy called out, just loud enough so she could hear.

"Yes, sir," she said. "How may I help you?"

"Me? Not so much," Freddy said. "My friend, Caz, here, needs your help desperately."

"Oh?" she giggled cutely.

"Caz went from school, where we knew one another, directly into the Rangers," Freddy explained. "He was an officer—a captain. For seven years, he's been out on the border, fighting the Rhetians. And you know what the saddest part is?"

"No. What?"

"Caz just confessed to me that he has no experience with women—at all," Freddy stated. "He was telling me that he thinks you are very pretty and that he wishes he could talk to you, but he has no idea of how to go about it. I was hoping you might find it in your heart to overlook the many mistakes he will undoubtedly make as he tries to get to know you better."

"Well, that's a relief," she said with a smile. "I thought you weren't interested, Caz. You would hardly look at me, and I was trying so hard to get your attention."

"Jenny, you're beautiful," I said in a whisper, my face glowing brightly from embarrassment. "It's all I can do to keep from staring, but I don't want to offend you."

"For not knowing what you're doing, what you just said is a pretty good start," she said. "Come back at half past nine tonight. That's when I'll be finished here. You can walk me to where I live and keep me safe. Will you do that?"

"I'd be delighted to, Jenny."

"Good. I'll see you then."

With that, she bent and kissed my cheek. More than just a peck, her soft lips lingered for a moment. I think my face turned an even more vivid shade of scarlet. Freddy laughed at my discomfort.

"You're welcome, Caz," he said.

"Freddy," I hissed. "Now what do I do?"

"That's easy," he said. "Show up here at half past nine, and let her teach you."

I showed up early. Can you blame me? I waited outside of the inn until I heard a nearby clock chime the half hour.

Jenny appeared a minute later. She wrapped a knit shawl over her shoulders as she approached. I offered her my right arm, as my grandfather taught me when I was only single digits in age.

Jenny clasped the inside of my elbow, and we crossed to the front door. I opened it for her. She stepped through and waited for me to give her my arm again.

We turned to the left. When we reached the end of the building, we turned to the left again. Behind the inn was a small stable. We stopped at a door on the end of the building.

"This is where I live," she said with a giggle. "Thank you for protecting me."

"You hardly needed my assistance," I stammered.

"Perhaps not," she teased, "but I've never felt safer."

Jenny turned to me and put her arms on my shoulders. She stood on tiptoe and pressed her lips to mine. I think my heart stopped beating as all my limbs froze.

"Your friend wasn't lying, was he?" she laughed. "Come on in. This will be fun."

Jenny took me to her small room above the stable. There were a dozen rooms. I learned later that they were all occupied by people who worked at the inn. No one saw us on the stairs or in the hall.

Jenny opened the door to her room and pulled me inside. She shut the door behind me and adopted the same posture as on the street. Her arms were around my neck, and she looked me in the eyes.

"Put your hands on my waist," she instructed.

I did as she asked. Her waist was small. I could feel the beginning of the swell of her hips.

"Cock your head just to the right," she said.

As soon as I did, Jenny mirrored my action. She raised herself up and touched her lips to mine. They were so soft. She held me like that until I was forced to break away in order to breathe.

"Breathe through your nose," she giggled. "You can kiss longer that way. Let's try again."

We pressed our lips together again. Jenny stepped closer, pressing herself against me from her knees to her chest. Her arms drew my head closer. She closed her eyes and hummed quietly. Her lips began to make subtle movements on mine.

I have no idea how long we stood like that. It was heavenly. All good things come to an end, and eventually Jenny pushed me away gently.

"Well done, Caz," she said, slightly breathless. "Come back again tomorrow night for your next lesson."

She opened the door and ushered me into the hall. After she shut the door behind me, I stood there, slightly stunned. Eventually, my wits returned, and I walked back to my rooms.

4

I won't go into the evolution of my "lessons" with Jenny. You can imagine how they progressed over the next few days. Let me just say that a week later, I understood for the first time in my life why my father forgot his station and engaged in relations with a pretty housemaid.

The next day, Freddy came to my rooms and told me my new clothes were ready. We went to his tailor, and I tried on my new finery. None of the pieces were as sturdy or practical as what Hamed Erdogan made for me, but they would convince someone that I was indeed a member of the landed nobility.

Freddy gave me a valise, and I packed for a stay of three days. In addition, he provided a small wooden chest containing three thousand ducats. I hailed a hackney in the square in front of the bookseller. Before going to the One-Eyed Cat, I stopped by the Brass Frog and told Jenny that I had business that would keep me away for the next few nights. She suggested I stop by midafternoon.

The hackney delivered me to my destination. Adopting the supercilious and snotty attitude I remembered Brantford Winstonworth displaying, I demanded the innkeeper fetch my bag and the chest. When he returned, I stipulated that I wanted the best room in the inn.

"Do any of your other guests play cards?" I asked the innkeeper. "I like a bit of a flutter now and then."

"We do have someone staying with us who might be interested," the man said. "I'll point you out to him at dinner. What brings you to the city, sir?"

"Milord," I corrected.

"Excuse me, milord," he said, knuckling his forehead.

"I'm here to settle my father's affairs and gain possession of his accounts," I said. "Do you have a safe?"

"We do, milord."

"Put my chest in the safe," I commanded, then watched as the innkeeper did just that.

Looking over his shoulder, I saw two other chests of similar size to the one Freddy gave me. One or both probably belonged to Tourville. I signed the register as "Brantford, Baron Winstonworth." That would certainly capture Sir Edmund's attention, as would my offhand comment about assuming control of the family finances. I felt certain I would receive an invitation to join a game of San-Sa that evening.

As I ate in solitary splendor that evening, a man approached. He was stocky, but his clothes were nearly as nice as what I was wearing. After he waited for me to swallow, he cleared his throat.

"Milord, excuse me for interrupting your meal. Please allow me to introduce myself," he said with a slight bob of his head. "Sir Edmund Tourville."

"Yes?" I replied after I looked him up and down with slight disdain.

"The innkeeper mentioned you might be interested in playing some cards this evening," Tourville said awkwardly.

"Oh. Yes," I said, giving him an obviously fake smile. "What are you playing?"

"San-Sa."

"Oh, very good," I said. "If you'd said Plafond, I would have been disappointed. Dull game, that."

"My friends and I agree," he said. "If you would like to join us when you are finished, we will welcome your company."

"What sort of stakes?" I asked.

"When things get especially heated, there might be a few thousand on the table," he said.

"Excellent," I said, rubbing my hands together in delight. "Will you require me to—"

"The innkeeper is holding your money along with ours in his safe," Tourville said. "We play using chips instead."

"And if things get, as you say, 'heated,' what then?"

"A bank draft the next business day is acceptable, with some sort of surety."

"Surety my ass!" I spluttered. "I'm Baron Winstonworth. That's all the damned surety you need."

"Of course, milord," Tourville backpedaled. "Your good name is all the guarantee required."

"I should hope so," I sniffed.

When I found the back room later, I met Sir Edmund's accomplices. They looked presentable, giving the appearance of prosperous business owners. Their names were unimportant as I was certain they were fake.

We played for several hours. I did not win every hand—that would have been too obvious. I did collect more than my fair share of the larger pots, though. Every time I won, I crowed—not the best display of manners. I made sure they knew I was spoiled and used to getting my way. That would help set the stage for the third night. The losses seemed to be spread evenly among my opponents. By the time we called it a night, I was over a thousand ducats to the good.

"Milord, please join us again tomorrow night," Sir Edmund asked.

"Ha!" I barked. "You want a chance to win your money back, do you? Sure, I'll come. You shouldn't expect to do any better, though!"

I'd already spotted some of their tricks. They were culling the cards, arranging for me to receive the occasional strong hand. I even caught the signal Sir Edmund gave to whoever was dealing and the rest of them. Following his gesture, all four of his cronies would stay in, bidding the stakes up so that I would win the larger amounts.

The other four were competent cheaters, but Tourville was the real artist. Culling cards was not terribly difficult when using an overhand shuffle. Managing to accomplish the same thing with a riffle shuffle took a much greater degree of skill. Sir Edmund was also skilled at deflecting attention with conversation while he handled the cards, seemingly absent-mindedly.

You might wonder how I knew what to look for. I honed my eye while at school, but I learned most of this from the armsmen in the March. Unlike the lessons supervised by my grandfather—such as dancing—they took it upon themselves to teach me. Knowing the steps to the Rufty-Tufty had not been of any use to me yet, but spotting cheaters had come in handy many times, both at school and in the Rangers.

The following morning, I rose early. When I walked outside, I hailed a hackney and rode to Freddy's house. Freddy's man, Roger, greeted me at the door and hollered back to Freddy that I was there. Freddy informed Roger that I would stay for breakfast.

I gave Freddy the recap of the events of the night before. He was dismayed that he had not picked up on their tricks. I explained that it was more difficult to spot a cheater when all the other players were doing it.

We arranged for Linc, Ratty, Paul, and RJ to be in the common room of the One-Eyed Cat. When things turned against me, as I expected they would, I would demand an outsider be brought in to act as the dealer. I was sure Tourville would agree. Freddy thought that Paul would be the best choice.

Sir Edmund would be confident in his skill at manipulating the cards and would not require the help of a dealer. At some point, he would muck a couple of cards and stash them away. When he received a hand where he could use them, he would. I would know because I knew the signal he would give to his cronies to bid the stakes up.

"Freddy, find a deck of blue cards and red cards that look similar to the ones you played with but have a slightly different pattern on the back. Give them to Paul. Have him switch decks when he joins us. Then tell him to look for my left eyelid to twitch," I said. "That will be the signal to switch back."

I returned to the One-Eyed Cat and demanded a hot bath. As long as I was playing the part of an entitled noble, I figured I might as well take advantage. By the time I finished and dressed again, they were serving lunch. After eating, I walked to the Brass Frog and up to Jenny's room above the stable. My "lessons" continued. Jenny said I was a brilliant student.

She shooed me away when she needed to get dressed and help with the dinner service. I walked back to the One-Eyed Cat. Sir Edmund invited me to join him for dinner. I accepted, acting as though I was doing him a favor.

"I didn't see you all day," he commented.

"It was extremely dreary," I whined. "Dealing with father's solicitors, gaining access to all of his accounts. The terms of his will are clear. I don't know why they have to fuss so much."

"They bill by the hour, milord," Sir Edmund said.

"Ha! That's it precisely," I laughed obnoxiously. "They bill by the hour, and once I gain control of that money, there will be no more hours for them."

"Did your father leave a substantial estate?" he asked.

"Of course," I replied smugly.

After dinner, we retired to the same room as the night before. I continued to win the hands with the greater stakes. At the end of the evening, I realized I was up nearly three thousand ducats. Again, they begged me to return the following night to give them the chance to win some of their money back.

"You can count on me," I said. "I'm nearly three thousand to the good and look forward to winning more tomorrow."

The highlight of the next day was my midafternoon appointment with Jenny. That evening, Sir Edmund insisted on dining with me. I noticed he encouraged me to drink heavily. Freddy had mentioned this as well.

We retired to play cards. The other men welcomed me warmly and thanked me for giving them the chance to win their money back. Unlike the previous two nights, I lost every hand where the stakes were high. They allowed me to win quite a number of deals when there was little money on the table.

All along, Sir Edmund encouraged me to drain my stein, and a refill was always prompt in arriving. I was nowhere near as drunk as he hoped, though. Someone more drunk or less experienced than I was might have been fooled into thinking everything was going well, but the diminishing pile of chips in front of me told a different story.

When we started two nights previously, I asked them to provide me with the equivalent of three thousand ducats in chips. Only a couple of hours in this evening, and I had less than two thousand in chips on the table in front of me. I'd lost my winnings from the previous two nights and a thousand more.

It was also clear that Sir Edmund was the big winner. The other four men were dangerously close to running out of chips themselves. I figured it was time to move things along.

"My luck seems to have turned," I said, over enunciating the way drunk people do, "but I am confident fortune will smile upon me again before the night is over. Does anyone have an objection to me buying another five thousand in chips?"

No one objected. In fact, Sir Edmund betrayed a slight smile. Three of his accomplices used my purchase of more chips as an excuse to leave the game, claiming it was too much for them. Sir Edmund counted out five thousand more in chips from a caddy on a side table and slid them over to me.

"Y'know," I said with a slight slur to my words, "with only three of us left, p'raps we should find someone else to deal the cards."

"Is it a matter of trust, milord?" Sir Edmund asked casually.

This was a clever maneuver on his part. He knew the Code of Honor as well as I did. If I made any sort of innuendo without proof in hand, he would have the right to demand a formal apology.

"Course not," I said airily, waving my hand carelessly. "It's just that the game is getting rather tense, and I think we would all be better off to let someone else deal so we can concentrate on our cards."

As I explained this, I stood unsteadily. I stumbled to the door and opened it. Sitting nearby were Ratty, Paul, RJ, and Linc, playing Plafond.

"Hey, you," I called out to them. "One of you c'mere and help us out. S'worth a hundred ducats to ya."

"This really isn't necessary," Sir Edmund protested as Paul Fassbender scurried over.

"S'alright," I said. "He's here already, and I promised him a hundred. C'mon in. You're gonna be our dealer."

"Um, right," Paul said. "What are you playing?"

"San-Sa," I said. "You know it, right?"

"Of course," Paul replied. "Um, these other two gentlemen don't seem to be interested in having me here."

"Well, if you don't stay, I won't either," I said petulantly. "I'll just call it a bad evening and get a good night's sleep before I head back east tomorrow."

This was the moment of truth. I was counting on Sir Edmund's greed. He and his friends won a thousand ducats from me—a substantial sum in my books—but there was the promise of so much more. I had roughly seven thousand ducats in chips on the table, and Sir Edmund wanted them all and then some.

"No, we'll allow this gentleman to deal for us," Sir Edmund said. "Let's keep playing."

We continued with Paul as our dealer. I played deliberately foolishly. My pile of chips dwindled.

Sir Edmund was clever. He allowed me and his remaining crony to win small amounts, just to maintain my interest. Neither of them noticed that Paul had switched the deck of cards we were using for one with a similar back. The color was the same, but the pattern of the design was slightly different.

I noticed that on two hands where Sir Edmund folded early, he only tossed four cards on the table. Paul caught my left eyelid flutter. He switched back to the original deck we had been using.

"I apologize, gentlemen," Paul said as he set the deck on the table, "but it is getting late, and I must be going. I hate to leave you in the middle of what seems to be a quite spirited contest."

"G'wan," I muttered darkly. "Ya didn't bring me any better luck, so good riddance."

Sir Edmund's accomplice dealt the next hand. I received good cards, but both my opponents folded early. It was now Sir Edmund's turn to deal, and I was sure he was going to arrange the deck to set me up for the killing blow.

True enough, he gave me a good hand—an almost sure winner—three and two, with queens over kings. It was eerily similar to the hand he'd dealt to Freddy. I allowed myself to smile at the thought, knowing that Sir Edmund would take my expression for happiness at my cards.

Sir Edmund's henchman stayed in long enough to bet everything he had, but when Sir Edmund raised, he shook his head and pushed away from the table. I had just enough to match Sir Edmund and offer a slight raise. I shoved all my remaining chips to the center of the table. Sir Edmund matched that amount, then counted out another five thousand ducats worth of chips and added them. He grinned at me.

"Wanna buy enough chips to see your cards, Sir Edmund," I said. "Another five thousand."

"I don't have any objection, Baron Winstonworth, but you did mention you were planning on leaving to head home tomorrow. Would you mind if I asked you for some surety?"

"I always make good on my debts, Sir Edmund," I said.

"I did not mean to imply otherwise," he said in an oily manner. "It's just…"

"What did you have in mind?" I asked.

"Your sword looks like a particularly fine piece of work," he commented.

"It was my grandfather's" I said.

"It would help me to sleep easier if you would leave that with me overnight," Sir Edmund suggested. "I'll be happy to return it to you when you bring me a bank draft for the ten thousand ducats."

"If you win," I snarled.

"If I win," he conceded.

"Fine," I snapped as I unbuckled my sword belt and laid it on the table. "But before we show our cards, Sir Edmund, do me a favor. Place them on the table, face down."

"What do you mean?" he asked, suddenly concerned.

"Place your cards on the table face down. I will do the same," I said, as I put my hand down.

As Sir Edmund went to do the same, his face went pale. He noticed, as I did, that two of the cards had a different pattern from the other three. I'd caught him cheating.

"Gentlemen!" I called out.

Linc, Ratty, Paul, and RJ came into the room quickly. I pointed to the cards on the table in front of Sir Edmund. All of them murmured disapproval at the sight of the mismatched card backs.

"Sir Edmund, I will give you a choice," I said. "Return Lord Rawlinsford's ring and his bank draft to me, and allow me to cash in my winnings, and I promise I will not breathe a word of what took place this evening—provided I never hear of you playing cards for anything more than friendly stakes again."

5

Not only had Sir Edmund tried to cheat at cards, he also cheated in allotting himself and his assistants more chips than they had money for. The two chests in the safe held just under twenty-five hundred ducats, and they were now mine. Even though it wasn't as much as it should have been, I thought it was a fairly profitable bit of work for three evenings of card-playing.

The next morning, after hailing a hackney and taking my two chests to Farmer & Mercantile and depositing the contents in my account, I returned to Freddy's house. I handed over his ring and bank draft, and the chest with the three thousand ducats he provided me. He was, as you might expect, thrilled. An even bigger surprise awaited me later when I joined him and the others for dinner at the Equestrian Club that evening.

"This is for you, Caz," he said, handing me a piece of paper.

"What's this for?" I protested when I saw it was a bank draft for five thousand ducats.

"You helped me avoid paying the full price for my foolishness," he said. "Nevertheless, I wrote a long letter to my father today, confessing my stupidity. Without your assistance, it would have been far worse. I figure you're entitled to half the value of my idiocy."

I tried to refuse, but Freddy would not hear of it. As I walked back to my rooms that evening, I marveled at my circumstances. In the city less than a month, and I now had nearly ten thousand ducats to my name. I had a nice place to live, new clothing, and met up with old friends.

On top of that, there was Jenny and her "tutelage." I certainly was an eager and attentive pupil. These lessons were far more interesting than anything I ever learned in school.

For the rest of the spring and summer, I was able to enjoy a life of leisure. I invited myself to Freddy's for breakfast a couple of times every week. He had me over to the Equestrian Club to play cards often. I visited the salle regularly and was as fit and healthy as I could ever remember. Freddy's father, the Duke of Manton, sent me a nice letter thanking me for helping Freddy.

The only cloud in my sunny sky was the end of my relationship with Jenny. We came to realize that while we enjoyed our time together in bed very much, neither of us had any sort of deep feelings for the other. Both of us decided at the same time that we should break things off.

One night, when I came over, Jenny looked troubled. That bothered me since I was planning on discussing calling an end to our dalliance. Our greeting was awkward.

"You look like something is troubling you, Jenny," I commented.

"Oh, Caz," she sighed. "I've been trying to think of a nice way to say this, but I haven't been able to find the right words. So, I'll just jump into it with both feet. I think our time has run its course."

Jenny was startled by my reaction. I laughed. Before I hurt her feelings, I pecked her cheek with my lips.

"Jenny, I reached the same conclusion," I confessed as I leaned back. "I was planning on breaking it to you gently tonight, but you—"

Jenny's laughter triggered my own. What could have been awkward and uncomfortable, the way these things usually are, ended up with the two of us laughing about it. We ended up spending one last night together and parted friends in the morning.

I was still trying to determine what sort of career I should pursue, but I will admit I wasn't worrying about it much. With the money I had in the bank and my non-extravagant lifestyle, I had enough for a decade or more of comfortable living. It was the middle of the month of Heyannir when I received a letter from someone named Pierre Luin. He asked me to come to his office.

Intrigued, I decided to follow through. His office was next to a solicitor's, in a small house that fronted a market square not far away. When I opened the door, a bell chimed.

"Who is it?" came a voice from what would have been the parlor.

"Casimir FitzDuncan," I replied.

"Oh! Mr. FitzDuncan. Thank you for responding to my inquiry so promptly," a man said as he entered the vestibule. "I'm Pierre Luin. Please—come in and sit down."

"How can I help you, Mr. Luin?" I asked after I sat across a sizeable desk from the man.

"I find myself in a spot of trouble," Luin said. "Lord Rawlinsford is one of my clients. He could tell something was bothering me and probed and probed until I confessed what it was. As soon as I did, he recommended I contact you. He felt you might be able to help me."

"I see," I responded noncommittally, wondering if Freddy was playing some kind of joke on me. "What is the spot of trouble you are in?"

"I'm being blackmailed," he said, his face flushing red with embarrassment.

"Over what?" I asked.

"Some letters I wrote to a lady several years ago when I was first married," he said.

"A lady who was not your wife, I take it."

"Correct, but please allow me to explain," he said hastily. "My wife and I are happily married—now—but that was not always the case. Our marriage was arranged by our families, and Maribeth's and my feelings were not a factor in the negotiations between our parents. There was a lady with whom I was involved before my marriage. I continued to correspond with her for two years after my wedding. The contents of the letters I wrote are quite … intimate. Someone reading them might infer that my relationship with the lady continued to be a physical one, though that was not the case."

"Is this woman the blackmailer?" I asked.

"Majors and Minors, no!" Luin exclaimed. "Her house was robbed a month ago. Among the things the bandits took were the letters I wrote. Ten days ago, I received a note that was slipped under the door. This note quoted some passages from the letters and informed me that it would cost me five thousand ducats to get the letters back."

"You say your marriage is on solid ground now," I stated. "Why not just confess to your wife—"

"I already did," he said. "A couple of years ago. Maribeth understands. She was not as indiscreet as I was, but she, too, left someone behind when we married."

"Then I don't see the problem," I said.

"It is not Maribeth," Luin stated. "It's her father. If he learned of the existence of these letters, he would break up our marriage and destroy my business."

"I don't understand," I confessed.

"I am a financier," Luin explained. "I manage money for people."

"What does that mean?"

"Instead of putting money in the bank, my customers give it to me," he explained. "I invest it in different things. For instance, there are a number of buildings here in the city that my investors own. The money from rents is then distributed to my investors based on what percentage of the property is theirs. We also own a variety of businesses, and, again, the profits are shared."

"What sort of returns do you generate for your investors?" I inquired.

"Between ten and twelve percent per annum," he answered.

"Seven Hells!" I gasped. "Farmer & Mercantile pays me just over one percent and acts as though they are doing me a great favor."

"They are doing the same thing with your money that I do for my clients," Luin stated. "They just keep the profits instead of passing them along."

"How could your father-in-law ruin you?" I asked.

"He was my first investor and is still my largest," Luin explained. "He and his friends account for three-quarters of the money I manage. If they demanded that I return their funds, I would be forced to sell just about everything immediately. It would be a disaster. I would be ruined."

"And there is no way you can explain things to him?"

"He is one of the most morally severe people I think I have ever heard of," Luin said. "He would never understand."

"Do you have the five thousand to pay the blackmailer?" I asked.

"Yes and no," Luin replied. "I would need to liquidate some of my investments to come up with the cash. My greater worry is that anyone who is a thief and a blackmailer is inherently untrustworthy. I have no confidence that this person would return the letters to me."

"Good point," I agreed.

"Mr. Luin, I will do my best to help you," I said after I thought for a few moments. "If I succeed, I will hand over the letters, and you will pay me twenty-five hundred ducats—over time, if need be. I have no desire to disturb your financial structure, but when I assisted Lord Rawlinsford—"

"He already warned me that your fee would be half the value of what was at stake," Luin said. "If you can get the letters back, it will be well worth it."

"You will also take me on as an investor," I stipulated.

"How much do you have to invest?" Luin asked.

"Ten thousand."

"You would be my smallest investor by quite a bit, but I will be happy to take you on," he said.

"Who is the lady friend in question?" I asked. "I will need to investigate the original crime to see if I can learn who your blackmailer is."

"Her name is Phoebe Saylor," Luin said.

"And she is not being blackmailed?"

"No. Her husband died last year," Luin said. "The blackmailer has no leverage with her."

"Do you have any objection to my calling upon her?"

"No."

"May I have the note that was left under your door?"

"Here it is," Luin said, handing it over.

"It's possible I may need more information," I cautioned. "If I do, I'll come back. Otherwise, I may not see you until I have the letters. How many of them are there, by the way?"

"Thirty. I wrote her once a month, beginning when I was betrothed and could no longer see her. In the last letter, I told her I would no longer keep writing, as Maribeth and I had grown to care for one another."

As I walked back toward my rooms, I wondered where to start in order to unravel Luin's problem. There was no signature on the note that was left. The sender was anonymous.

I reckoned the logical point at which to begin would be with the City Watch. They were in charge of public safety in the city. Their responsibilities were crimefighting and firefighting.

Passing through my market square, I continued on, heading to the Palace of Justice. This massive building housed the courts and the City Watch. I figured I would start at the top, and ask to see Sir Oliver West, the Principal of the Watch.

He would probably hand me off to an underling, but Sir Oliver's involvement would gain me more cooperation than I would expect otherwise. Starting at the bottom rung would get me nowhere. I didn't expect to learn much regardless. As far as Pierre Luin knew, the City Watch had not solved the case. Given that a month had passed, I doubted they ever would.

As I walked, I realized I needed to come up with a ruse. Simply showing up bald-faced, and demanding to see Sir Oliver would result in me being escorted out of the building promptly. Seeing a handbill stuck to a post, I snatched it, rolling it into a tube. I would claim I was ordered by one of the magistrates to deliver this important document to Sir Oliver's hands.

When I reached the Palace of Justice, I went to the administrative entrance. There was a long hall, lined with portraits. I learned later they were former Principals of the Watch.

At the end of the entrance corridor was a bored-looking clerk at a desk. I marched right to him. When I stopped in front of him, he looked up wearily.

"Yes?"

"I have an important document for Sir Oliver," I said with authority.

"I'll take it," he said in a disinterested manner.

"The magistrate ordered me to put it in his hands myself," I responded.

"Fine. You know where his office is?"

"No."

"Up the stairs and to the left," he said, jerking his thumb over his shoulder at the door, already having turned his attention away from me.

I walked past quickly, surprised at how easy this was. The stairs were right there. I climbed them two at a time, then headed left.

There was only one office there. Sitting behind the desk was a man who looked to be in his early forties. His black hair was turning gray at the temples. He looked up when I knocked.

"Sir Oliver?"

"Yes?"

"My name is Casimir FitzDuncan," I said as I entered.

Sir Oliver gave me a puzzled look. I shut the door behind me. Then I took a seat in one of the chairs in front of his desk.

"What brings you here, Mr. FitzDuncan?" he said, betraying growing annoyance.

"I would like to ask you a few questions about the burglary that took place at the home of Phoebe Saylor a month ago," I said.

"Why?"

"I'm looking into a related matter for a friend," I said.

"You'll need to give more than that, Mr. FitzDuncan."

I weighed carefully what I could tell Sir Oliver. Pierre Luin would not want word of his problem to spread. By the same token, Sir Oliver would not be in his current position if was unable to keep a confidence.

"Sir Oliver, please understand that this is a sensitive matter. My friend would appreciate your utmost discretion."

"I understand."

"Thank you. Among the items stolen from Phoebe Saylor were some letters written by my friend years ago. If those letters were shared with certain people, my friend would be ruined. The burglar realized the importance of these letters and left an anonymous note under my friend's office door. He is demanding five thousand ducats for them."

"Ah! Blackmail. That makes the case more interesting," he said.

"It was not interesting before?" I asked.

"Not particularly," he admitted. "A robbery of a wealthy widow's empty house is unfortunate but hardly earth-shaking."

"Empty house?"

"Maid's day off, and Madam Saylor was out," Sir Oliver said. "Whoever it was moved quickly. They took her jewelry and as much of her silver as they could easily carry. It probably took less than a quarter of an hour."

"And you have no idea who did it?"

"I never said that," Sir Oliver replied in a slightly testy tone.

"Oh? You know who did it?"

"There are six men we know of who we believe could have done it."

"Why have you not arrested them?" I asked.

"Because it would serve no purpose," Sir Oliver stated. "Without more certain knowledge, a magistrate will not grant me the authority to execute a search of his premises."

"Then how will you catch them?"

"At some point, they will have an accomplice try to sell some of the loot. We will attempt to apprehend this person and, through him, find the burglar."

"That does not sound like a foolproof method of catching the criminal," I observed.

"It's not," Sir Oliver admitted, "but it's the best we can do. I have only so many on the Watch. If we don't catch them in the act, it becomes much more difficult."

"Would you be willing to share the names of your primary suspects with me?"

"What will you do with the information?"

"It is probably better that you do not know," I admitted.

"You're not contemplating violence, are you?"

"I hope to avoid it," I said.

"You'll have to pardon me, Mr. FitzDuncan, but I have no idea who you are. Is there someone of repute who can vouch for your character?"

"Would Lord Rawlinsford be a suitable reference?"

"He would."

"Please feel free to ask him about me," I said. "And when you are satisfied, will you provide me with the names?"

"I will consider it."

6

There was nothing more to be gained from this meeting. I thanked Sir Oliver for his time and apologized for my subterfuge in gaining access to him. He asked where I lived in the event he wanted to contact me. I left the address with him.

From here, my next stop would be the widow Saylor. I expected to learn that she kept the letters in the same place as her jewelry. With her husband dead, she no longer needed to hide them. They clearly meant something to her, or she would not have kept them, and were important enough to her that she noticed their absence immediately.

I wondered briefly if her maid might be a lead to the burglar. Since the idea came to me so readily, I quickly dismissed it. Sir Oliver struck me as a shrewd individual. His ready knowledge of the circumstances of the burglary indicated to me that he would have considered that possibility already and investigated it. Nevertheless, I made a mental note to ask him when I saw him next.

As I walked, I heard the clock chime one o'clock. My stomach rumbled in recognition of the hour. Happily, it was Freyday—a market day in the city. That meant there would be food vendors in every market square. Since moving into the city, I discovered one of my great weaknesses. The kind of delicacies prepared by vendors in carts made me salivate. Meat cooked on a skewer, dough fried in oil and then drizzled with honey—these were culinary delights that pleased my stomach and my soul. I stopped and ate, standing in the open air, on my way to visit Madam Saylor.

The widow Saylor's maid was a saucy little thing. She was barely five feet tall, with light brown hair, hazel eyes, a spray of freckles across her upper cheeks, and a nose with a slight upturn at the tip. She obviously watched me coming up the short walk from the street, as she opened the door as soon as I knocked.

"How may I help you, sir?" she said in almost a purr, looking up at me through long eyelashes.

"Is Madam Saylor in?"

"Who should I say is calling?" she asked, her tone now slightly teasing.

"Casimir FitzDuncan," I replied, handing her one of my calling cards. "She would not know me. I am a friend of a friend. He asked me to look into the recent burglary."

"Oh! Of course, sir," she said. "Please step inside, and I will fetch madam."

When the maid walked away, it seemed to me she was putting some additional swish to her hips. My thought was confirmed when she looked over her shoulder to see if I was watching. When she saw that I was, a naughty smile turned up the corners of her mouth.

The widow Saylor appeared a minute later. She was an attractive woman. I guessed her age at somewhere on the near side forty. It was difficult to tell, so I based my estimate more on how old I thought Pierre Luin was. She certainly looked too young to be a widow already.

"Yes?" she said.

"Madam," I said with a small bow. "A mutual acquaintance asked me to look into the recent burglary. May we speak in private?"

"Certainly," she said. "Sally, we will be in the parlor. Would you please prepare some refreshment for our guest? It is quite warm today, and I imagine he must be thirsty."

Sally the maid curtsied, saying, "Yes, ma'am."

Madam Saylor gestured toward the parlor to my left. I opened the door for her and followed her in. She sat while I shut the door behind me.

"Pierre Luin asked me to—"

"Oh!" she gasped. "Oh, dear! I am so sorry to have brought such trouble upon him."

"You know the robbers are trying to blackmail him?" I asked.

"Yes," she said. "A few days after the robbery, I stopped by his office to warn him the letters were missing. He told me he had already heard from the criminals."

"May I ask where you kept the letters?"

"In my jewelry box," she said. "After Pierre wrote the last time, I tucked them all away. I married less than a year later, and before you ask, my marriage was a happy one. The letters lay at the bottom of linen drawer, and I forgot all about them. When Jason died—"

"Jason was your husband?" I asked.

"Yes. He was older, you know—considerably older. Like Pierre, ours was an arranged marriage, but it might as well have been a love match. Jason treated me like a queen, and I adored him."

"If it's not too forward of me, may I ask how he died?"

"The doctors suspect it was a tumor. He fell ill, and never recovered. He just got sicker and weaker. It took him in less than a year."

"I'm sorry for your loss," I said sincerely.

"About three months after the funeral, I started going through Jason's things, preparing to get rid of them. That prompted me to want to do a more thorough job, and I decided I would clear out everything that hadn't been touched in a few years. You're young, so you wouldn't know, but you will be surprised to find out how many odds and ends you accumulate year by year. Anyway, I opened the chest and came across Pierre's letters."

"And decided to keep them?"

"Mr. FitzDuncan, I was in such a low state," she explained. "I missed Jason terribly. Reading Pierre's old letters reminded me of a happier time."

There was a quiet knock on the door. Sally came in a moment later, bearing a tray with what looked to be a pitcher of lemon squash. She set the tray down and poured two glasses. After handing one to her mistress, she turned to give me mine. She bent at the waist, giving me a delightful view of her décolletage. I'm only a man, and I looked—a bit longer, perhaps, than is polite. She rewarded me with a smirk.

"Will there be anything else, ma'am?" she asked after she straightened.

"No, Sally. Thank you."

Sally went to the door. I watched her twitch her hips as she did. When she left, I was embarrassed to see Mrs. Saylor smiling at me.

"She has weekends off, Mr. FitzDuncan," she said.

"Oh, my," I said with a slight groan of embarrassment. "I apologize, madam. That was quite inappropriate of me—"

"Not really," she laughed. "You are presumably a normal, healthy male. Sally was clearly advertising her interest in you and her availability. She is very pretty, as you are quite handsome. You would have needed supernatural ability to resist her display."

"Still, it was—"

"Pish-posh, Mr. FitzDuncan," she said. "You are a handsome devil. If I were ten years younger, I would find an excuse to show you my bosom and shake my behind as well. The two of you put a smile on my face for the first time since the burglary. If you don't ask her if you may call on her, I will be disappointed."

"I would hate to disappoint you, madam," I said in a teasing tone.

I took a sip of the lemon squash. It was quite good. There was just enough sugar added to soften the sourness of the lemon without removing the tartness.

"Then don't," she replied with a grin. "So, Pierre asked you to help get his letters back?"

"He did. I helped a mutual friend recover something valuable in a situation where the law could not help, and he gave my name to Mr. Luin."

"And the law cannot help now, can it?" she observed.

"That appears to be the case," I said. "I met with Sir Oliver West before coming here. He has a short list of suspects but cannot do anything until they try to sell some of the things they stole. With the money they hope to extort from Mr. Luin, it might be a couple of years before they find it necessary to take that step."

"Does Sir Oliver know about the letters?"

"He does," I admitted. "But he is a gentleman *and* the Principal of the City Watch. He will not give me the names of the suspected burglars until he checks up on me. I believe we can count on his discretion."

"Pity," she said. "A bit of scandal might make this old hag more attractive."

"Madam, you are not old. Neither are you a 'hag.' If I may skirt the bounds of propriety, I will say you are a beautiful woman."

"Thank you, Mr. FitzDuncan. I wasn't fishing for compliments but appreciate yours all the same. The problem is the distinct lack of bachelors my age. I shall keep hoping, though. So, what will you do?" she asked, changing the subject.

"I'm still gathering information," I said. "Once I know more, I will have an idea of what the next steps should be."

"Well, one of your next steps should be to ask Sally if you may see her on her day off tomorrow," she said with a naughty smirk.

"As you wish, madam," I replied.

"Sally," she called out. "Please see our guest to the door."

"Madam, it has been a pleasure to make your acquaintance," I said as I stood.

I crossed to her and took her hand. Bending over, I pressed my lips to the back of it gently. Behind me, I heard Sally sigh.

"Miss Sally, your mistress suggested I should ask if I may call on you tomorrow, as it is one of your days off," I said. "Would you permit it?"

"I think I would prefer it if you offered to get me out of the house," she said. "The weather promises fair, and I would enjoy fresh air and sunshine. Come collect me at eleven. Use the back entrance so we do not disturb my mistress."

"Very well," I said. "I shall look forward to seeing you then."

As I did with Madam Saylor, I took Sally's hand and kissed the back of it. When I released it, I backed through the door, waiting for her to shut it. Her eyes were sparkling as she did.

I will admit I had a spring in my step as I headed back to my rooms. The prospect of spending the day with Sally was a pleasant one. I started thinking of how we could spend the time enjoyably. She said she craved fresh air and sunshine, so I stopped by the livery and made arrangements to rent an open buggy for tomorrow.

I knew where I would take her. There was a small lake just outside the west gate of the city. The land belonged to the crown and it was open for public enjoyment. I thought I should pack a lunch for the two of us, but preparing food was not something I considered a strength.

After the livery stable, I wandered to Freddy's. Roger answered and hollered back that I was there. Freddy yelled in return to let me in.

"Caz, you're just in time," Freddy said from his usual position sprawled on the sofa. "I was just wondering what sort of trouble I should get into tonight. Care to join me? Roger, pour us some sherry, will you?"

"Freddy, I need to ask a favor of you," I said. "Of Roger, actually."

"Sure, Caz. What do you need?"

"I'm taking a young lady out for the day tomorrow," I explained. "I've arranged for a buggy and thought we would spend the day at the lake. We'll need lunch, and I was hoping—"

"Roger, will you please put together a lunch for Caz and his lady friend for tomorrow?" Freddy requested.

"Wine, milord?" Roger asked.

"Of course, include the wine," Freddy said. "Glasses, too. There. Done. Tell me about this girl."

I explained to Freddy who she was and how we met. Since Freddy was part of the group when I met Jenny, it had been no secret that I was seeing her. He knew none of the details, though. Similarly, I knew Freddy was dallying with a young woman named Patricia. I had not met her yet.

This was all fun and games for Freddy. When the time came for him to marry, he would be matched up with someone from either a noble or wealthy family. My prospective bride would be someone like Jenny or Sally, who is of no particular family. That didn't mean I couldn't enjoy myself now. Marriage was years in my future, I hoped.

"Do you have any idea how to go about helping Pierre?" Freddy asked.

"I have two notions," I said. "One depends on Sir Oliver releasing the list of burglary suspects to me. By the way, I gave him your name as someone who would vouch for my character."

"I have not heard from him yet, but will be happy to speak on your behalf," Freddy said. "So, what are you thinking?"

"If he provides me the list, I can learn more about them, then perhaps attempt to steal the letters back," I said. "If he will not give me any names, or does not give them to me soon enough, I may need to pay the ransom and identify the culprit that way."

"And then rob the robber," Freddy said.

"Exactly. Pierre says he cannot afford to pay five thousand ducats, so I may need to," I explained.

"If they want the money in coin, that will be a heavy chest," Freddy pointed out. "Five stone or thereabouts. They may ask for a bank draft, in which case you can fake something."

"The problem with that is they probably have already entertained the same thought," I said. "Neither of us has a criminal bent, Freddy, and we both thought of that immediately. No, I reckon they'll demand coin."

"That should make the person easier to follow, at least," Freddy remarked.

"Perhaps. Tell me, Freddy. If you were going to pick up a chest with five thousand ducats and get away clean, would you choose a crowded place or somewhere with no people around?" I asked.

"Hmm. The problem is the weight of the chest," Freddy said. "It would take two men to carry it for any distance, or they would need to have a cart of some kind nearby. Perhaps on a market day, it would be possible."

"Where if you ask for the ransom to be delivered to a large empty space," I suggested, "it would be easy to see anyone waiting and watching to see who would pick up the loot. You would be able to detain them and prevent them from following. So, which would you choose?"

"I suppose it depends on how patient our blackmailer is," Freddy said after he considered the question for a few minutes. "Arranging for the transfer to take place in a busy market square would be the quickest. It would not be too hard to create some sort of distraction that would hinder any pursuit and allow you to begin your escape. On the other hand, with so many people about, things might not go smoothly. People might see you with the chest and remember you."

"Where if you ask for the chest to be taken to the middle of an open field, you can watch from a distance and see if there is anyone lingering behind to catch you," I suggested. "The blackmailer will, of course, stipulate that if he spots anyone keeping watch over the ransom, the deal is off, and the threatened consequences will follow. That will force anyone watching to stay at a considerable distance. The blackmailer can then come in once darkness falls and take the chest away."

"You've convinced me that the second option is safer," Freddy said. "Fewer things that could go wrong, and I would have more control over the situation. How would you foil his plan?"

"I'm still thinking about it, Freddy," I admitted. "Right now, I have some vague ideas, but whether they will work or not depends on the circumstances of where he wants the ransom delivered."

"If it were me," Freddy said, "I would pick a fallow field or one with only vegetables. At this time of year, any sort of grain would provide too much cover for someone trying to hide from me."

"That's a good point," I agreed. "That being the case, I would demand that the chest containing the ransom be delivered a couple of hours after sunrise. That way, I could observe to make sure no one stayed behind—even though there is nowhere to hide."

"What if the blackmailer does not provide delivery instructions until after sunrise?" Freddy inquired.

"Then I will have a difficult time getting my money and the letters back."

"I will call upon Sir Oliver in the morning," Freddy said. "I'll bring the list back with me."

"If any of them live in the Kettle, I'll need a map," I said.

"I'll get that, too."

Since moving to the city, I wandered extensively all over, except for the area known as the Kettle. It was an area in a bowl-shaped declivity between two hills that reached to the river. In addition to the kettle-shape of the land, it was the hottest area of the city during the summer months. The surrounding hills prevented any sort of refreshing breeze from reaching it. That might have been another reason for the name.

As you might expect, it was section of the city where the poorest lived. The style of building was slapdash. Everything was mashed together and there was no consistency in the materials used. Most of the buildings resembled a house of cards. The only obviously sturdy building was the one belonging to the City Watch. It was made of thick brownstone.

People who lived in the Kettle were different from the rest of the city. Because of the widespread poverty, they disliked and mistrusted everyone else. None of the residents cooperated with the City Watch. They had a distinct accent, and their own slang, incomprehensible to outsiders. A trooper in my unit in the Rangers came from the Kettle and tried to explain the slang to me on a couple of different occasions. I never did understand it.

Addresses throughout the city were haphazard. In normal neighborhoods, though, if you could not find a house, you could ask a resident, and they would help you. That would not necessarily be the case in the Kettle. I would need a map.

7

Despite our best intentions, Freddy and I were reasonably well-behaved that night. We enjoyed a nice dinner that Roger cooked. After we ate, both of us were so comfortable, we decided not to go out. I returned to my rooms and heard the clock in the square ring ten as I got into bed.

The next day was my appointment with Sally. At midmorning, I collected the buggy from the livery stable. I drove it to Freddy's house, where Roger gave me a basket after he explained what he made for our lunch. He had also included a nice blanket for me to spread out for the two of us to sit upon.

As instructed, I arrived at the rear entrance of Madam Saylor's house at eleven. Sally came out before I did much more than climb out of the buggy. She was dressed in a fetching cream-colored dress, wearing a broad-brimmed hat and white kid gloves. The clothes looked rather fine for a maid to own.

"Madam Phoebe gave me the clothes," Sally said when she noticed me looking as I helped her into her seat. "She wanted me to look my best for a handsome man like you."

"Well, you look quite fetching," I said. "The dress fits well and the color suits you."

"You look quite dapper yourself," she said, commenting on one of the suits Freddy bought for me to play Baron Winstonworth. "Where are we going?"

We spent an enjoyable afternoon. I found us a shady spot and spread out the blanket. We shared the delicious lunch Roger prepared for us and chatted away, learning more about one another.

At one point, we fell silent. Sally gave me a look I learned to recognize with Jenny, and I leaned forward and gave her a kiss. That led to quite a few more, though that was the extent of our play.

We returned to the city in the later afternoon. I contemplated asking Sally if she would like to have dinner with me but decided against it. We'd spent enough time together, and I did not want her to grow tired of my company. She allowed me to kiss her cheek when I walked her to the doorstep. From the corner of my eye, I saw the curtain of a nearby window pulled back slightly. Madam Saylor would have plenty of questions for her maid.

I had to respond to an inquisition myself when I returned the basket and blanket to Freddy's house. That ended up turning into an invitation to dinner at the Brass Frog. Despite Freddy's interest, I told him very little of my afternoon.

It was not much past nine in the morning on Maniday when I heard someone banging on the door. I opened it to find Freddy. He strode in with a big grin and handed me a piece of paper. There were six names on it.

"Do you have the ratty clothes you once told me about, Caz?" he asked.

"I think Placida has been using them for dust rags," I said.

"Find them, and put them on."

"Why?"

"Sir Oliver is going to have one of his watchers show you where each of these people lives," Freddy said. "You need to look like you belong in the Kettle, or you'll draw suspicion."

I managed to find a shirt and a pair of breeches. Both were dirty. Placida had indeed been using them to clean.

"Perfect," Freddy announced when I held them up. "Get dressed—no stockings, no jacket, and leave your sword here."

Freddy hailed a hackney outside, and we rode to the Palace of Justice. Bypassing the clerk at the end of the entrance corridor, Freddy went through the doors to Sir Oliver's study. Sir Oliver looked up at Freddy's knock. He saw my attire and nodded.

"Dennis!" he yelled.

A moment later, a man dressed just as shabbily as me appeared at the door. His hair and beard were also unkempt. Sir Oliver pointed at me.

"This is the man."

"Come along then," Dennis said.

I left Freddy behind and followed Dennis out of the building. We set off on foot toward the Kettle. He didn't say anything until we were almost there.

"Let me see the list again," he demanded. "What do you want with these guys?"

"Someone robbed the home of a woman and stole some letters," I explained. "They are using the letters to blackmail a friend of mine."

"And you want to get the letters back? What about the other things they took?"

"I only care about the letters," I said. "Sir Oliver can deal with the other things."

"Good choice," Dennis agreed. "That makes things easier—in and out quick. It also narrows down your list to two."

"How?"

"Only two of these guys are smart enough to have grabbed the letters in the first place," Dennis said. "The other four wouldn't touch anything that didn't shine or glitter. And of those two, one is more likely than the other. Tell me, can you handle a knife?"

"I'm more used to a sword, but I can fight with anything," I said.

"Fair enough," Dennis replied. "Do you have one?"

"Nothing other than kitchen knives."

He bent over and pulled a knife from inside his boot. The blade was not quite ten inches long, fixed into a wooden handle. It had no guard.

"Tuck that away. I'll show you Dinker's place first."

I hid the knife in my boot, as Dennis had done. He knew exactly where he was going. We twisted through the narrow streets of the Kettle until we stood across from a ramshackle building.

"This is Dinker's house. He's the one I would bet is your blackmailer."

"Are we going inside?" I asked.

"No," Dennis said dismissively. "You're going to come back tonight. If you show up around ten, chances are good he won't be home. That's what you want. Have you ever broken into someone's house before?"

"Of course not," I replied.

"Seven Hells," Dennis muttered. "Fine. Listen carefully. Now, you see the hole under where the latch is bolted on the inside of the door?"

"Yes."

"You need to bring a hook to fish the latchstring out," Dennis explained. "That will get you inside. Be quick and quiet. If no one is right there to see you, stop and listen. Make sure you don't hear anyone. If you don't, head up the stairs. They'll be right there."

"You know this?" I asked.

"Yes. I've been inside," he answered. "Now, when you go up the stairs, put your feet on the very edge of the treads. That lessens the chance of making noise. Same thing when you get upstairs—stay next to the wall. The first door you see will be a room filled with stuff Dinker is looking to sell. His bedroom door is toward the front of the house."

"And you think he would have the letters in his bedroom?"

"I'm almost certain of it," Dennis said. "Open the door quietly. There's a chance he might be asleep in bed, though I doubt it. He likes to drink too much."

"Where in the bedroom should I look?"

"Nine times out of ten, you'll find a loose floorboard under the bed," Dennis explained. "All these guys think they're so clever, and they all use the same hidey-hole. Lift the floorboard and feel around."

"What if it's not there?" I asked.

"Then you'll need to work," Dennis said. "Pull out every drawer and dump them on the floor. Fish through the contents. Check if any of the drawers have a false bottom. Be swift but thorough. Time is not your friend."

"Fine. Where's the other person's house?" I asked.

"I'm not going to show you," Dennis said. "You survive this adventure and come up empty, stop by tomorrow, and I'll show you the other place. Either way, bring my knife back to the Palace of Justice, will you? Unless you're dead, in which case you'll owe me."

We headed back the way we came. We exited the Kettle and found ourselves in a better part of the city. Dennis clapped me on the shoulder.

"This is where we part, friend. Good luck tonight."

"I'd feel more confident if you would help me," I admitted.

"No question," Dennis said with a chuckle. "I can't, though. Sir Oliver explained that we don't have enough of a reason to search Dinker's place, and the City Watch can't take the law into its own hands. You're just a guy—not part of the government. You can do something we can't. Plus, if someone suspected I was there, I wouldn't be any good to the Watch in the Kettle anymore."

I headed back to my rooms and changed back into normal clothing. After wasting the day, reading a book I borrowed from the shop, I went to the Foaming Boar for dinner. When I finished, I returned to my rooms and changed back into my disreputable clothes.

An hour after darkness fell, I left and headed to the Kettle. I found the rickety-looking house. The door was latched from the inside. I stuck a small hook through a hole drilled just under the latch. When I pulled it back, there was a leather thong. I tugged on the thong, and the latch clicked open.

I stepped inside. When I was clear of the door, I stopped and shut it. The room was completely dark.

After standing in complete silence, my eyes adjusted to the gloom. I started up the steps leading up to a second floor. Placing my feet carefully at the edges of each tread closest to the walls of the stairway, I crept upward.

When I reached the top of the stairs, I stayed close to the wall as Dennis instructed. The door nearest the stairs was slightly open. I could see a variety of objects but no bed. I headed toward the front of the house to the next door.

I stopped and pulled the knife from my boot. Though I had heard nothing, people asleep can be pretty quiet. I counted down from three to myself, then threw my shoulder into the door and burst through. No one was in the bed. I breathed a sigh of relief.

I dropped to my hands and knees. It took me some feeling about, but I soon determined that there was indeed a loose floorboard. More scrabbling got my fingertips a purchase on it, and I was able to lift it and reach underneath. The first thing I felt was a ledger book. I pulled it out and slid it behind me. Then my fingers touched what I hoped were the letters.

They were rolled up, and it seemed as though the bundle was bound by a ribbon. I pulled them out and squirmed from under the bed. In the very dim light of the room, I looked and confirmed I had what I sought. After I set them down, I moved back under the bed to see what else I could find in the hidey-hole.

The only other thing I felt was a leather bag. It was heavy when I lifted it. That was a good sign. Satisfied there was nothing else hidden, I replaced the floorboard. I picked up the bundle of letters and counted them quickly. When I reached thirty, I breathed a sigh of relief.

On my way out, I did not keep to the edge of the corridor or the stairs. Both squeaked loudly. Reaching the front door, I cracked it open. This gave me a chance to see if there were any passers-by who might notice my exit. Satisfied that I would be relatively unobserved, I opened the door all the way and stepped out.

I continued on until I reached my rooms. Once there, I threw the clothing I'd been wearing back into the bin where I found it, and undressed for bed. I also took the time to examine the contents of the heavy purse I took. It held over four hundred ducats.

In the morning, after cadging a free breakfast from Freddy in exchange for telling him of my adventure the night before, I went first to the Palace of Justice. I wanted to return the knife to Dennis and hand the ledger to Sir Oliver. From my brief look at the book, the thief kept track of what pieces he gained from each robbery. I was certain it would be useful to the City Watch. Sir Oliver agreed.

"Thank you, Mr. FitzDuncan," he said as he examined it. "It's so helpful when concerned citizens hand over items of interest such as this. Why, this information gives us a good reason to call on this individual and see if he is in possession of said goods."

"I'm afraid I don't really understand what you just said," I admitted.

"The courts will not allow the City Watch to search someone's house unless we have a verifiable reason to do so," he said. "If we observed this Dinker fellow with one of the stolen items in his hand, that would be enough. It's also not likely to happen. They know the rules and how to skirt around them. If one of my people went into his house and retrieved this ledger, the court would throw any charges related to it out. Since you, a private citizen, turned it in, we can use it to enter his house."

"Then I'm happy to be of assistance," I said. "Will you also please return this knife to Dennis?"

"I'll be happy to. Now, if you'll excuse me, Mr. FitzDuncan, I need to organize a squad to go visit Mr. Dinker's residence."

I returned to my residence to pick up the letters to deliver them to Pierre Luin. Lyle Forteney saw me approaching and went to the door to flag me down. I walked over, wondering what he wanted.

"There's a gentleman waiting for you upstairs," Forteney said.

"A gentleman?"

"He claims he's the Duke of Manton," Forteney said.

"Oh, my!" I said.

I hurried to my entrance on the side of the building. The duke is Freddy's father. Freddy mentioned he was writing to his father about his peccadillo. I guessed his father had questions for me. When I opened the door, he was sitting in my customary spot.

"Your Grace," I said, slightly breathless from charging up the steps.

"Hello, Caz," he said as he rose to greet me.

"Um, welcome to my humble abode, Your Grace," I stammered as I bowed.

"Caz," he tsked. "You are an adult now, and a friend of the family. I insist that you call me David."

"Yes, Your—David," I fumbled.

"I wanted to thank you personally for helping Freddy with his indiscretion," he said. "He is lucky to have a friend like you. I've thought that ever since he brought you home with him ten years ago."

"I'm the lucky one," I said.

"Freddy wrote me, you know, and shared all the details. I have only one problem with how the matter was resolved. He should have given you the full amount of his foolish wager. I wanted to set that right," the duke said.

He handed me a piece of paper. It was a bank draft for five thousand ducats. When I read it, my hand started to shake.

"Your Grace, um, David," I stammered. "This is too generous. It's an enormous sum of money."

"Don't tell me you can't accept it, Caz, because if you try, I will be quite cross with you. You helped Freddy learn a valuable lesson. It could have been far more expensive except for your involvement. Now, sit down and tell me what you have been doing since you left the Rangers."

I did, still clutching the bank draft. The duke had always been kind to me. When Freddy brought me home with him for the summer, the duke accepted me as part of the family. In fact, Freddy's whole family treated me as one of them. The circumstances of my parentage didn't matter to them at all.

David wanted to know all the details of how I dealt with Sir Edmund. When I finished with that, he then asked about my current undertaking. I shared with him that the matter would be resolved as soon as I delivered the letters to Pierre Luin.

He asked how Luin was going to compensate me. I shared that we agreed on half the amount the blackmailer was demanding. David gave me a thoughtful look.

"You know, Caz, you are providing a unique and valuable service," he said. "I can't tell you how many times I have heard of someone being cheated or tricked, or even—more rarely—blackmailed as Pierre was. The law usually cannot help these people. You can. Look at you—less than a year out of the Rangers, and you've already earned over ten thousand. If you keep at this, you'll be able to retire comfortably in ten years."

"I don't know how many people there are that need someone like me," I said.

"Nonsense," he stated. "I already know someone who needs to contact you—Sir John Dunleavy."

"What happened to him?" I asked.

"He was cheated quite badly in purchasing a horse," the duke said. "That's all I'll share. The rest is his story to tell."

"Well, thank you, Your—David," I said.

"You know, when Freddy brought you home, it pleased me in a way that is difficult to explain," he said. "The Austermain and the Barry clans have always been friends and allies."

"I'm not a Barry—" I started to say.

"Yes, you are, Caz," the duke spoke over me urgently. "You are a Barry in every way that counts—particularly in your strength of character. One of these days, I'll get Duncan to pull his head out of his ass … never mind. There are some things you'll learn more about when the time is right, Caz. For now, let me just say that I consider your father a friend, estranged for a couple of decades, perhaps, but still a friend—once a very good friend, as you are to Freddy."

8

After the duke departed, I headed to Farmer & Mercantile, and deposited the bank draft he had just given me. I then asked for a draft for ten thousand ducats. This, I would give to Pierre Luin to begin my investments with him.

With the new draft and the bundle of letters in hand, I went to Pierre's office. When I entered the vestibule, he called out that he was speaking with a customer, and asked me to wait. Roughly ten minutes later, a distinguished looking gentleman exited Pierre's office. As he opened the door, I held the bundle of letters behind my back. The man looked familiar, but I could not place him.

Needless to say, Pierre wore a very anxious expression upon seeing me. He had not seen the bundle behind my back. For all he knew, I was coming to tell him the job was impossible. He gestured for me to come into his office.

When I stepped through the door, I presented the letters to him. The look of relief on his face was almost comical. He stood speechless for a moment.

Suddenly, he gave himself a shake, like a wet dog. He crossed to the small stove in the corner of the room. Stooping down, he opened the door and put some of the letters inside.

"I don't care how warm it is," he said, striking sparks from a flint. "I need to destroy these immediately."

The spark caught on the paper, and Pierre blew gently, coaxing it into flame. As the flame took hold, Pierre began feeding the letters in one at a time. After he added the last of them, he stayed in a crouch until he was satisfied that it was completely burned up.

"Thank you, Mr. FitzDuncan," he said. "You have saved me."

"Please, call me Caz," I requested.

"Pierre," he responded.

"Pierre, as we discussed, I would like you to invest some money for me," I said as I handed over the bank draft. "You told me that I am your smallest client, but—"

"Caz, the amount invested might be the smallest, but my debt of gratitude will make you my most important client," he said with sincerity. "I have an idea I would like to mention to you, as far as the other compensation to which I agreed. Instead of cash, which would require me to sell off pieces of different businesses, would you accept twenty-five hundred ducats worth of ownership in different ventures?"

"Pierre, I would prefer that over cash, now that you bring it up," I said.

"Excellent," Pierre said. "Give me a moment. Let me look through the books and pick out a couple of the more attractive properties for you to review."

"Pierre, that won't be necessary," I said. "If the Duke of Manton trusts you with his money, I have complete confidence in your judgment."

"You honor me, sir," Pierre said humbly. "Thank you. Once I determine where I will invest your money, I will issue a statement. For now, I will write out a receipt for twelve thousand, five hundred ducats."

On Njordday, four days later, I hailed a hackney in the market square just in front of the bookshop. I gave him Phoebe Saylor's address. Tonight, I was taking Sally to an early dinner and then to see a play.

The hackney delivered me to the rear entrance of the house. Before I reached the door, Sally opened it. She gestured for me to come in.

"Madam wishes to speak with you," she whispered.

I gestured to the driver to ask him to wait, then followed Sally inside. She led me to the parlor where I first met her employer. As the door opened, Madam Saylor stood and crossed to me quickly, enfolding me with a hug.

"You dear, sweet boy," she said.

I stood there awkwardly, not knowing whether I should return her embrace. With Sally standing there, it was doubly uncomfortable. In addition, I did not know why Madam Saylor was so emotional.

"Sir Oliver West came to call on us yesterday afternoon," she said. "He brought back everything that was stolen. All my jewelry, all the silver—everything except the letters. He explained that you had those."

"I did and gave them to Mr. Luin," I said.

"Good," Madam Saylor said emphatically. "Thank you. I was not expecting to see any of my things again, but I am delighted to have them back. My late husband gave me the nicest pieces of my jewelry, and they have value to me far beyond any monetary value. I am exceedingly grateful."

"I am happy to have been of service, madam," I said gallantly.

"Spoken like the gentleman you are," she said. "I don't wish to keep you. Sally tells me you are going to dinner and a play. Go. Have a wonderful evening."

We did have an enjoyable evening. Dinner was good, and the play was amusing. The only disappointment was saying goodbye later. Sally tried to entice me in, but I would have been too embarrassed if Madam Saylor knew. We agreed that Sally might spend the night with me at my place in a week. That certainly gave me something to look forward to.

The next morning, I invited myself to Freddy's for breakfast. His father was still there, planning on beginning the journey home after he ate. Before he left, the duke reminded Freddy to introduce me to Sir John Dunleavy. Freddy invited me to join him for lunch the next day at the Equestrian Club.

When I arrived the next day, the maître d' showed me to a table. Freddy was there with Linc Ellsworth and a man I did not recognize. I figured he would be Sir John. It turned out I was correct.

We enjoyed our lunch and played plafond afterward. I was paired with Sir John, and we had a spirited game. The cards treated all of us evenly, and all four of us were skilled. Three hours later, when we totted up the score, Sir John and I won a florin each. It was one of the closest games I could remember having.

Freddy and Linc excused themselves, claiming they had other commitments. I suspected they were just leaving so Sir John could tell me why he might need my help. We moved to a table in the corner of the room, away from other guests.

"The Duke of Manton speaks highly of you," Sir John said. "He is the one who suggested I meet you to see if you could help me. I learned how you assisted Lord Rawlinsford, but my problem is entirely different."

"Without knowing more, I can't say whether I can be of assistance," I said.

"Right. Well, the fact of it is, I was cheated. There is a man who raises horses on the near side of Eatonford."

"Eatonford?" I asked, not having heard of the place.

"A ride of seven days north and east of here," Sir John said. "The man's stable is half a day's ride short of Eatonford."

"Sorry," I said. "Please continue."

"This man, Samuel Comegys, breeds horses," Sir John said. "In the past, his horses were nothing special—just useful, well-mannered mounts. Recently, he entered one of his mounts in a steeplechase near my holding. It's a day's ride west of his place. Anyway, the horse, Gallant Warrior, won the race by a huge margin. I discussed with Comegys whether he would consider selling the animal to me. Comegys said he would let me know."

Sir John paused his narrative when a server came to inquire if we wanted anything. Dunleavy ordered us both a glass of sherry. When the server departed, he resumed his tale.

"We exchanged letters. He offered to sell me the horse for twenty thousand ducats. Based on what I saw in the race and from my superficial inspection of the animal, that was a reasonable price for such a fine steed. I obtained a bank draft and sent my head groom with it to Comegys."

Our sherry arrived then. Sir John paused his account. The server waited until Sir John tasted the sherry and approved. Sir John nodded and waited for the man to depart.

"When my man returned, the horse he had was most definitely not the one I saw at the race," Sir John said. "The markings were the same—a white blaze on the nose and chest—but it was a horse that was average at best, worth no more than two or three hundred ducats. My groom told me that he argued with Comegys, knowing that I would never have agreed to pay such a sum for this animal, but got nowhere. Comegys claimed this animal was Gallant Warrior, and the markings were exactly as he described in his letter agreeing to sell me the horse."

"What did you do then?" I asked.

"I rode over to see Comegys myself, bringing the horse with me. We nearly came to blows. I demanded to see every horse in his stable, thinking I would be able to spot the one from the race," Sir John said. "He allowed me to view them, but only from a distance. None of them had the white blaze on the forehead that I remembered. One looked like the horse I'd seen, but without the markings. I demanded to see it more closely. Comegys then had his men force me from his property."

"Have you discussed the problem with a lawyer?" I asked.

"Of course," Sir John replied. "He said that my complaint will go nowhere as far as the courts are concerned."

"By any chance, in the exchange of letters with Comegys, did you mention that you would send your head groom to collect the horse if Comegys agreed to sell it?" I asked.

"You know, I think I did," Sir John said, smacking himself on the forehead. "That was stupid of me, wasn't it."

"Not if you were dealing with an honorable man," I said.

"No, it was stupid," Sir John said. "Horse traders are not well-known for their ironclad ethics."

"What sort of resolution are you hoping for? Would you like your money back, or the horse?" I asked.

"The horse," Sir John stated.

"What else can you tell me about this man, Comegys?"

"He has no reputation for breeding racehorses," Sir John said. "Up to the race I saw, no one could remember him entering one of his horses to run. When I checked with the race steward, he mentioned that there were a handful of bets placed on Gallant Warrior that day. Unknown animals typically start at three hundred-to-one odds. By the time the race started, it went off at seventy-to-one."

"That sounds interesting," I said. "How much was wagered?"

"The steward told me there were five bets, totaling two hundred ducats," Sir John said. "They paid off fourteen thousand."

"Majors and Minors!" I gulped.

"Of course, knowing what I do now, I'm convinced the man cheated," Sir John said. "It's certainly not unheard of for a long shot to win a race, particularly out in the country, but…"

"I wonder where he obtained the animal?" I mused.

"That's something I tried to investigate as well," Sir John said. "None of the breeders I know would admit to doing business with him. Only one had ever heard of him before."

"So, Comegys cheated on the race, then defrauded you for good measure," I observed. "I wonder if he's finished."

"What do you mean?"

"Between the race and swindling you, he has over thirty thousand ducats. Is that enough for him, or will he try for more?" I asked.

"I wouldn't have any idea," Sir John stated.

"I apologize," I said. "That was more of a rhetorical question. I wouldn't expect you to know."

"It's pretty obvious to me what Comegys did," Sir John said. "I have no doubt that the horse currently residing in my stable is named Gallant Warrior. The horse he entered in the race, and the one I thought I was buying, is a different animal. Comegys used white paint to create the markings on the nose and chest. Shame on me for not realizing it."

"Wouldn't you have been able to detect it when you looked at the horse after the race?" I asked.

"If he'd used paint, certainly," Sir John said. "I imagine what he applied was more in the nature of boot polish—that sort of consistency and adhesion. It wouldn't cake up, like paint. If he put it on carefully, in repeated applications, it would be almost impossible to detect. I was much more focused on other aspects of the horse's anatomy, not the markings."

"I see. How much longer do you plan to stay in the city, Sir John?" I asked. "I need to think about how to go about this."

"As long as you need me," he replied. "I was planning on leaving at the end of the week."

"I should have some ideas before then," I said. "Where are you staying?"

"At the Parkview," he replied.

The Parkview Inn was perhaps the nicest in the city. It was originally built overlooking a large section of open land. The land was not a park, though the locals called it one. The owners sold it parcel by parcel, and buildings gradually covered most of it. The inn bought the last remaining empty lot across the street. That was all that remained of the "park."

"And you are aware of my terms?" I asked.

"Yes. The duke told me half the value. In this case, ten thousand ducats," Sir John said. "It will make this horse the most expensive I've ever owned. Still, it will be worth it to me. It's the principle of the thing. I can't stand that someone was able to cheat me. I don't want anyone to know about it."

I left the Equestrian Club and headed for my rooms. As I walked, I pondered a number of loose ends to Sir John's problem which I could grasp. The steeplechase season had just started. I reckoned Comegys planned on entering the horse under other false names at other races out in the country.

That was a crime which the equestrian community took seriously. Racehorses that ran in steeplechase events were registered with an organization known as the Grand Chase. Comegys's horse was probably registered when he bought it. Entering it under a false name would affect the integrity of the races, something the Grand Chase took great pains to safeguard.

Sir John's interest in buying the horse was unexpected. Comegys probably would have refused to sell if he thought Sir John would come to collect the horse himself. Reading that Sir John would send his groom gave Comegys the opportunity to cheat—an unexpected windfall.

My best chance of connecting with Comegys would be at one of the races. He would probably stay away from the capital. Instead, he would enter the horse in more far-flung locations, trusting that any communication from one venue to another would be too late to catch up with him.

How to approach him was another question. I did not know enough about breeding to pass myself off as someone like Sir John. Nor did I have the sort of resources where I could pose convincingly as an owner. I did know enough about horses from my upbringing and time in the Rangers that I would be a believable itinerant groom.

Finally, I needed to think of a way to get the horse to Sir John. This was potentially the most dangerous part. Stealing a horse was a hanging offense in the kingdom. I wondered what the penalty for switching one for another was. My intention was to avoid being caught, of course.

My footsteps took me to the Foaming Boar since it was near dinner time. From our years together in the Rangers, I knew Carl Stensland possessed good common sense. If I described the problem to him, he would be able to poke holes in it and make suggestions, just as he did on the western border.

Fortunately, it was a slow night. I was able to convince Carl to join me at my table. Once he sat down, I explained the situation to him—without using any names, obviously.

"How did this come to you, Cap'n?" he asked.

I explained in very broad terms how I helped Freddy and Pierre Luin. Carl listened attentively. He asked probing questions that forced me to tell him more than I initially intended.

"This is what you do now, Cap'n?" he then asked.

"What do you mean?"

"Help frogs hop out of the pot before the water comes to a boil—when no one else can?"

"That's an interesting way of putting it, Sar'nt," I said. "I suppose so."

"You'll need help—accomplices, I guess you could call them," he said with a grin. "I agree that simply stealing the horse is too risky. If you get caught, even with Sir John to speak for you, it doesn't change the fact that you're a horse thief. Switching one for another will keep you from getting hanged—maybe."

"Your cheerful outlook on my prospects for success is heartening, Sar'nt," I remarked.

"The way I see it, you need two people to help you," he explained. "Someone nearby with the horse you plan to switch in for the one you take, and another person to be your go-between and help you pull off the switch. Get your—what do you call him, a client?"

"That's as good a word as any, I suppose."

"Get your client to lend you two of his grooms."

9

I headed to the Parkview Inn the next morning. To be honest, I went early enough that I hoped Sir John would buy my breakfast. He did. As we ate, I explained what I planned to do.

"I'll arrive at the site of a race looking for work," I said.

"The race venue will hire you," Sir John confirmed. "They always need more people for the days leading up to a race. These places usually only hold the one race each year. The course will need work, and the stalls will need to be mucked. It's not glamorous, but it will get you in the right place."

"I need some helpers," I said. "One needs to be nearby with Gallant Warrior. The other needs to be able to be my messenger. And you'll want to cover the markings on the horse with boot polish or whatever will best disguise him."

"I can free up two of my people for this," Sir John said. "You'll need the race schedule."

After we ate, Sir John suggested we go to the Equestrian Club. They had information on every horse race scheduled to be run throughout the kingdom. There was an event scheduled in Whinage in less than two weeks. I mentioned that I doubted whether I could get there in time.

"Nonsense," Sir John said. "We'll take my carriage and leave tomorrow. Whinage is eight days away, so you'll get there in plenty of time."

"It would be best if no one saw us together or even near the same place at the same time," I said. "If you would drop me a day's walk from the town, that would give the proper impression."

"We can do that," Sir John agreed. "I'll have to get one of my grooms there a couple of days later. A second man will bring Gallant Warrior and encamp nearby."

"Make sure the second man has a large jug of whiskey," I said. "I'll need it to be able to switch the horses in the middle of the night."

"Planning on getting everyone drunk? Good idea. Will you be using your own name?"

I hadn't thought about that. It made good sense not to spread my own name around. If this Comegys figured out who did it, I certainly did not want him to find me.

"Ralph Hubbard," I said, deciding quickly on a name.

I pronounced "Ralph" as "Raff," the way they did back east. Having grown up in the Eastern March, I knew the accent. It would be easy for me to adopt it as "Ralph."

"Very good," Sir John said. "I'll have my man on the lookout for you when he arrives."

"Sir John, there is no guarantee that Comegys will be at Whinage," I said. "If he does not appear, we'll just need to go to the next event."

"That gets trickier," Sir John said. "The next weekend, there are two steeplechase races. One is fairly near Whinage, in Allroyd. The other is much further east, in Carmarthen."

"And after that?" I asked.

"Again, two events—one in the west and one in the east."

"Comegys does not want to try his trick in events close to one another," I reminded him. "If he does not run in Whinage or Allroyd, we should be able to expect him in the next one in that area."

"Jeffer's Ford," Sir John said.

"Excuse me?"

"The next race near Allroyd will be in Jeffer's Ford. That will also be the last race in that part of the country for three weeks."

"Well, if we don't run into Comegys in Whinage, Allroyd, or Jeffer's Ford, then we will need to reevaluate," I said. "He may have given up on his scheme or perhaps even been caught."

"What will you do then?" Sir John asked.

"Reevaluate," I said with a bit of cheek. "I think our plan is sound. We can't help it if Comegys doesn't play along."

We parted, with Sir John telling me he would collect me outside the bookseller's in the morning. Leaving the Equestrian Club, I went in search of a second-hand clothing store. I headed in the direction of the Kettle. The part of the city where I was would not have any shops like this.

If I were going to play the part of an itinerant groom, I needed to look like one. Even my shabby clothes that Placida was using for cleaning rags would not do. For one thing, they were not constructed with sturdy enough materials. I needed working man's clothing.

A few blocks away from the Kettle, I spotted what I was seeking. The shopkeeper looked at me warily. My current mode of dress was not what he was used to seeing on his customers.

I found three shirts—more like tunics due to their length—and three sets of pantaloons. All were made of homespun wool. Though they showed clearly that they were by no means newly made, I judged they still had lots of wear left in them. I selected three pairs of short stockings, also made from homespun, and then examined the boots.

My current boots were too fine. I needed something more crudely made. They also needed to fit well. I would be doing lots of walking, and blisters would be an unacceptable impediment. The eighth pair I tried on was the first that fit comfortably. I didn't stop, though. After I tested every pair that seemed to be the right size, I narrowed it down to the eighth pair and the eleventh.

Both seemed nearly equal in comfort. I then examined the soles and the stitching. After looking at them, I admitted to myself that I didn't really know what to look for.

"If you needed to buy one of these pairs of boots," I asked the shopkeeper, "and knew you had many miles to walk, which pair would you pick?"

He came over and picked them up, one at a time. He looked at the same things I did before handing them back. His face bore a frown.

"If yer doin' a far piece a' walkin' yer gonna wanna get new soles on this pair," he said, indicating the second of the two I'd chosen.

"Why the one and not the other?" I asked.

"These bin re-soled two, three times a'ready," he said, pointing at the first pair. "T'others hain't bin but once."

I thanked him for his advice. The total for all the clothing and the boots was three florins. I think the shopkeeper expected me to haggle with him, but I needed to get the boots re-soled that day and didn't want to waste the time. Instead, I let him feel he'd taken advantage of me. He smirked when I paid without making a counteroffer.

In the market square where I lived was a cobbler. I took the boots to him and asked if he could put new soles on right away. He paused before answering. I suspected he was considering how much he could get away with charging me more than whether he could get the job finished in time.

"Two florins," he said.

"Done," I agreed, fishing the two coins from my purse. "I'll be back before five o'clock."

After I dropped my newly purchased clothing back at my rooms, my next stop was Madam Saylor's house. Since I would be gone for several weeks, I did not want Sally to think I was ignoring her. She met me at the rear entrance when I arrived. We had planned for Sally to spend the night at my place in a few days. I could only hope she would be as disappointed as I was.

"What brings you here, Caz?" she asked with a smile.

"Sad news, I'm afraid," I said. "I have a—a client," I said, using the term Carl used, "who has a job for me that will take me out of the city for a few weeks. It is important business, and I must go. I wanted to let you know so you did not think I was neglecting you or avoiding you."

"Oh," she said, her disappointment showing on her face. "When will you return?"

"It will probably be near the end of Twiman if all goes well. I'm sorry."

"That's a month away," she said in a sad tone.

"I know. It's a fair bit of traveling. I'm sorry," I said.

"As am I," she replied with a pout. "There are other young men who have asked me out. I have been putting them off, you know."

"I'm sure someone as pretty and as charming as you are, Sally, would have plenty of men interested in seeing more of you," I said, a bit glumly. "And I know a month is a long time."

"Well, when you return, you may call on me," she said with a slightly bitter tone. "Perhaps we will see more of one another. Perhaps not."

With that, she shut the door in my face. That had certainly not gone as well as I hoped. As I walked back to my rooms, I considered her reaction. It was a bit more selfish than I anticipated. I knew so little about the fairer sex that I had no earthly idea if her behavior was normal and if I deserved to be treated this way. The only person I could think of who might be able to share some insight with me was Jenny. I decided I would go to the Brass Frog for dinner that evening.

There were three more things I wanted to obtain before setting off on this adventure. I could not take my sword. It was far too fine for someone who was essentially a vagabond. I needed a decent knife. And since I would be walking quite a distance between races, if Comegys was not present at Whinage, I would need a waterskin. On the walks, chances were that I would sleep in the open, so a blanket would be necessary.

I needed to go to a number of different shops before I found what I sought. When I had the different items, I returned to my rooms and made a bindle using the blanket to hold all my stuff. I needed a staff so I could carry the bindle over my shoulder. The only thing I could find was a broom. I took it apart and left a note with a couple of florins, asking Placida to buy a new one.

It was a slow night in the Brass Frog. After I finished eating, Jenny was able to sit with me. I shared not only the details of this afternoon's conversation but the progress of my relationship with Sally thus far.

"Should I be reading anything into her reaction?" I asked Jenny that evening.

"She sounds a bit spoiled and immature," Jenny said. "How old is she?"

"Twenty."

"It sounds to me like she has some growing up to do and some mistakes to make," Jenny said. "And you'll be happier if you're not in the middle of it. I think she will do one of two things while you are away. If she really cares for you, she'll wait for you to return and won't see anyone else while you're away."

"And, if not?" I asked.

"She will go out with other men while you're gone, then try to rub your nose in it when you come back, hoping to make you jealous," Jenny said. "My advice to you if she takes that path would be to break things off right then. Perhaps she will come and apologize. If she does, you can certainly forgive her, but you'll be much happier if you don't take up with her again."

I frowned.

"Caz, it won't be your lesson to learn," Jenny said. "Sally needs to know that it's not right to play those kinds of games with the emotions of others. If she doesn't face any consequences, she'll never learn. Of course, she may never learn regardless—some people don't—but it won't be your fault. And you'll be much happier without the drama. It's not like you will lack for interested female companionship."

"What do you mean?" I asked.

"Come on, Caz," Jenny sighed. "How long after we called it quits did it take before you met Sally?"

"I don't know," I said. "A couple of weeks?"

"Exactly," Jenny laughed. "Caz, you're young, handsome, and charming, and carry yourself like a gentleman. You will have no difficulty in finding someone new if things don't work out with Sally."

In addition to my "work" clothes, I also packed a valise with clothing suitable for sharing a carriage with Sir John. We would be on the road for eight days. I did ask him if he would hang on to my nicer things until the job was finished.

After a week of travel, we reached the town before Whinage. I spent one last night in a comfortable bed in the inn. In the morning, I changed into my homespun, left my bag with Sir John, and set off on foot to Whinage.

It was four leagues away. On foot, it would take me half the day to cover the distance. I grabbed a loaf of bread from the inn, filled my waterskin at the well in the center of town, and set off with my bindle over my shoulder. When I arrived in Whinage that afternoon, I asked where the race would be held.

"Well, I can point you in the right direction," a man said, "but there's no one there just yet. They'll start getting everything ready tomorrow. Horses will arrive later in the week. You looking for work?"

"Aye," I replied.

"They always need extra hands," he said. "I'm sure they'll take you on if you give them a fair day's labor."

"Never heard no one complain," I said, using my eastern accent.

"Take the road east," he said. "About half a league down, you'll see the stands and the barn. They only use the course for the one race a year. There's a lot of work to get it ready for the race."

The site of the course was easy to spot. When I reached the barn, I dropped my bindle and went to explore. I started in front of the stands.

From looking at them, I could see there were a number of planks that would need to be replaced. I walked along the rail marking the inside of the course. Sections of it were broken or rotted. The grass along the entire course needed to be cut. The hazards, filled with water for the race, were instead full of muck and scum. The fences over which the horses would jump were in poor condition. Almost all of them would need to be repaired.

After I made the complete circuit, I went in the barn. It seemed to be in better condition than the race course. Even so, I could see holes in the roof and some siding missing from the walls. My prospects for employment were good.

I returned to Whinage and found an inn. Upon entering, I humbly asked the innkeeper how much he would charge for dinner. He took a look at me, and a deep sniff.

"You can eat in the kitchen for a demi-florin," he said.

I knuckled my forelock. Then I fished in my purse, pulling out smaller copper coins to make up a demi-florin. Before I quite had enough, he stopped me.

"That's fine, son. Go eat. You're here to help get us ready for the race?"

"Aye," I responded, keeping my eyes down.

"I'm sure they'll be able to put a fine lad like you to work," he said, patting my shoulder.

After I ate, the cook gave me a loaf of bread to take with me. I filled my waterskin and returned to the site of the race. Once there, I spread my blanket and waited for darkness to fall. It began raining in the middle of the night, so I picked up my things and moved into the barn.

It was still raining when I woke. The loaf of bread the cook gave me the night before served as my morning meal. I did not need to wait long before I heard people arrive.

I wrapped my things back into a bindle and propped them with my staff in the corner. There was a group of three men standing in the light drizzle, obviously discussing needed repairs. I approached to where they would notice me but kept a respectful distance.

"You there," one of them called.

I pointed to myself dumbly.

"Yes, you," he said with mild exasperation since there was clearly no one else he could have been addressing. "Are you here to work?"

"Aye," I answered. "Hopin' ya need me."

"What can you do?"

"Anything, sirs," I said. "I'm good with horses, too."

"None of the horses will be here for at least three more days," he said. "But there is plenty to do before they arrive. We can pay a florin a day."

"Thankee, sirs," I said. "I'm yer man, then. Jes tell me where ya want me to start."

"What's your name, son?"

"Ralph Hubbard."

"Well, Ralph, we need to make a list of the materials we will need before we can get started on repairs. In the meantime, the course needs attention," he said. "You'll find tools in the shed behind the barn. There's a scythe. It'll be dull and rusty after sitting all year, so you'll need to sharpen it. Once you do, we need you to cut the grass on the course, then rake it up."

"Aye," I said and headed off to find the shed.

I found the shed. At first glance, there were almost all the tools I would need. The scythe did need attention. It took some searching before I found a whetstone. Once I did, I set about sharpening the blade. It did not take long.

With the scythe, I headed back to the course and began cutting the grass while the men were still there. They seemed pleased that I started working immediately. I knew how to swing the scythe, but the last time I used one was years before when I was still in school. The two summers I spent at school, they put me to work in exchange for housing and feeding me.

With a sharp blade, the grass was easy enough to cut. I was using muscles that I had not exercised in a long time, and they began to let me know it. On my hands, I could also tell that I would have blisters soon. Taking a break for some water, I went to look in the shed for a pair of gloves. I found some, and they seemed in fair condition. With any luck, they would help keep the blisters from forming.

10

I worked hard for the next three days. By the end of the first day, I'd mown the course and raked the cut grass away. The next day, I shoveled all the muck from the water hazards and replaced it with clean water. After that, I worked with the three men in repairing the inner and outer course rails and the fence obstacles. We also replaced any suspect planks in the stands.

Though they had not mentioned it, they fed me as part of my wages. Each day a different man's wife brought us lunch and dinner. We all ate heartily, having worked up appetites.

The afternoon of the third day, other people showed up to work. We expected the horses and their owners to arrive the next day, so we set about cleaning the stables. When we finished the stables, we attacked the grounds. Overhearing one of the local men in charge addressing me as "Ralph," one of the newcomers approached me. He was very short and slight.

"Dick Franklin," he said, extending his hand. "I was told to look for you."

"Nice to meet you," I said quietly. "We probably shouldn't spend too much time together. Perhaps we can talk after dark."

"Understood," he said.

That night, Dick Franklin and I managed to get away from the other workers briefly. He confirmed he was one of Sir John's grooms. We discussed different ideas for what we would do if Comegys showed up.

"When the owners arrive, where do they stay?" I asked.

"The owners usually stay in the local inn or as guests in someone's house," Dick said. "Their grooms and jockeys will usually sleep in the barn, near the horses."

"Do many of them bring jockeys?" I asked.

"To an event like this? Not usually," he replied. "The groom they bring will usually be a boy—one who is good with horses but hasn't hit his growth yet. He'll also serve as the jockey. Usually once they start to grow the owner lets them go."

"Unless they are your size?" I asked.

"Even I'm too heavy," Dick said with a chuckle. "I'll ride to help train the horses, but not in a race."

"It sounds cruel to simply let these boys go," I commented.

"Maybe," Dick said with a shrug. "It's just the way it is."

"I think we should make the switch in the middle of the night," I said. "When we do this, we need to make sure everyone is asleep. You have a friend not far away?"

"I do. He has the horse we will switch in."

"And you know where to find him?" I asked.

Dick nodded.

"Does he have a jug of whiskey?"

"He does," Dick said, nodding. "Getting everyone drunk—especially the boys—will make sure everyone sleeps soundly."

"Figure out how to get it from him," I said. "We'll break it out the night before the race. All the hard work will be done, and it gives us an excuse to celebrate a little."

The next day the owners and their horses arrived. To my disappointment, Comegys was not one of them. Dick and I discussed it. He decided to leave before the race. The men in charge had asked me to stay until the morning after, to help clean up. I would then walk to Allroyd.

The race was well-attended, drawing over a thousand people from nearby communities. For me, the best part was the food. I've already confessed my love of the kinds of delicacies prepared in these sorts of food carts. Even better, the cost was within the budget of even a poor man such as Ralph Hubbard.

One of the two favorites won the race, so plenty of people went home happy. I began picking up trash as soon as everyone cleared out. The next morning, I mucked out the stalls in the barn. The men in charge let me go in the late morning. They said the work was done, paid me the full wage for the day, and told me that I would be welcome to come back next year to work. I knuckled my forelock, put my bindle over my shoulder, and set off down the road to Allroyd.

It rained most of the two days I spent walking. I arrived at the race course outside of Allroyd in midmorning, a day later than when I came to Whinage. The men who made up the local race committee were already there. I asked for work, and they accepted. The first job was to clean the stables, which were not mucked out after the race the year before. When I finished that, I began cutting the grass on the course. The condition of the fences and rails was better in Allroyd, but the barn needed more work.

I spent more time repairing the roof of the barn than I did on the race course, but otherwise, the pace of the work was similar. Two days later, other men showed up, with Dick Franklin among them. We quickly finished the repairs to the barn that the locals wanted.

The day before the race was when the horses and their owners arrived. I tried not to pay attention, but I was hoping Comegys was among them. Dick Franklin caught my eye later and laid his finger beside his nose. I nodded in recognition of his signal.

When we finished work for the day, I wandered through the barn to look at the horses. I didn't linger in front of any of the stalls. The tag on the stall of the one named "Meadow Flier" said the owner was Samuel Comegys. "Meadow Flier" was brown except for a white sock on his right foreleg. While I only had a brief glance, "Meadow Flier" appeared to be a handsome animal to me.

"Can you check the foreleg?" I whispered to Dick Franklin when we had a moment by ourselves.

"Already did," he muttered quietly back. "It's not paint, but that horse doesn't have a white foreleg."

"I thought it might be something similar to boot polish," I said.

"Something close to that," Franklin agreed. "My friend will leave the jug behind the shed later today. There are enough people coming and going that no one will pay attention to him or see him do it. He'll bring 'Gallant Warrior' to the shed about three hours after it gets dark."

"Is there any chance he can—"

"Put a white sock on 'Gallant Warrior' to make it look the same?"

I nodded.

"He's already doing it. We're using chalk mixed with a very soft wax. It should be close to whatever Comegys uses," Dick said.

"Will it escape detection?"

"Probably not, but I also have an anonymous letter for them to find. The letter states that Comegys entered a registered horse under a false name at the steeplechase in Polan," Dick said. "He cheated the bookies out of fourteen thousand ducats and was planning to do the same here. That will provoke a lack of sympathy for Comegys, I think."

"Has Sir John learned more about the horse he thought he was buying?" I asked.

"He learned where the horse came from. Comegys bought it from a breeder near Newcastle. The horse's real name is Mystic Mirror, and he is registered with the Grand Chase."

"What about the ownership question?" I asked.

"Once we get Mystic Mirror away from here, Sir John has a letter he will deliver to the Grand Chase explaining how Comegys switched horses. The letter will ask them to investigate the other races Comegys has entered this year. Sir John's lawyers are confident he will be granted ownership of Mystic Mirror. Just to be safe, we're taking him somewhere else until the question is settled."

After bringing dinner to us, the locals who made up the race committee left. Only the workers and grooms remained. As had been the case the week before, the grooms were all boys, right around the age of twelve or thirteen, I reckoned. We were all sitting around a small fire.

"With all the work done, we should celebrate," Dick Franklin said.

"With what?" one of the other men asked.

"Give me a minute," Dick said. "I'll be right back.

When he returned to the fire, he was holding a good-sized jug. The other men recognized it for what it was and began to smile. One laughed out loud and clapped his hands.

"There's plenty for all, lads," Dick said as he uncorked the jug and, balancing it on his forearm, tilted it to his lips.

"Ah!" he said when he lowered it.

The whiskey made its way around our circle. The boys needed to be taught how to hold the heavy jug. All of them coughed after their first taste. When it got to me, I understood why.

Though I held the jug up to my lips for what would appear to be a decent drink, I allowed only a taste to enter my mouth. This stuff was strong. The others would be passed out drunk before we finished half of it.

The boys were the first to succumb. Goaded on their elders, they showed no moderation. A few of them crawled away and we heard them retching in the dark. The others simply keeled over where they were.

I felt some guilt for the ones who vomited and went to check on them. When I stood, I made sure to wobble and stagger, to act as drunk as the others probably felt. All four of the lads who had crawled away were sleeping soundly, which I announced to the group.

The men found that hilarious. They continued to pass the jug from one to the other. None of them refused. Soon enough, two of them were nodding where they sat. The other man stood.

"I gotta take a piss," he said.

Dick and I watched as he stumbled away from the fire. A moment later, he heard a thud. Dick went to investigate.

"Out cold," he said with a grin.

It was less than an hour later when we heard a quiet whistle coming from the direction of the shed. Dick got up and headed over. I found a stick and lit one end of it in the fire to use for light, and went to the door of the barn.

Dick showed up a minute later, leading "Gallant Warrior." We switched the two horses, and Dick led the one we knew as "Meadow Flier" into the darkness. He returned to shake my hand.

"It's good to know you, Ralph Hubbard," he said, "or whatever your name is."

"Thanks, Dick, or whatever your name is," I replied. "Tell your boss that I'll begin walking to Jeffer's Ford after this."

"Will do. Good luck," he said quietly as he slipped into the darkness, carrying the jug with him.

I stretched out next to the fire to sleep. Dick and I decided that it would be best for him to disappear. When the organizers of the race appeared in the morning, they would find all the workers and the grooms sleeping off a drunk. They would, of course, ask where the whiskey came from. Having the one who procured it be missing was appropriate.

Later, Samuel Comegys would discover that his horse had been switched. He would raise a stink and demand to question all of us. None of the others would know a thing about what happened in the middle of the night. I could plead ignorance just as well as they. He would know Sir John was behind it as soon as he looked at the animal more closely.

The next day started with a bit of a ruckus when the organizers came to the site and found all of us still asleep. Their unhappiness grew as it was immediately apparent that all of us stank of whiskey, and our appearance displayed all the characteristics that follow a night of heavy drinking. Even worse was that the boys began throwing up as soon as they were woken. If I hadn't needed to pretend I was as hungover as the others, I would have been laughing pretty hard. The scene was comical.

What would add to the humor was watching the boys ride in the race in a few hours. They were all as sick as could be. Bouncing on horseback would see all their stomachs churning again. The Allroyd steeplechase this year would be a memorable race indeed.

The clamor rose to a new height when Comegys arrived and discovered that his horse was not the one that he had brought to Allroyd. All of us were lined up and questioned. We all pleaded ignorance.

"It's clearly the one who brought the whiskey and then disappeared," Comegys shouted. "I demand that you begin a search immediately for that horse thief!"

"Mr. Comegys, we have only your word that this is a different animal," Tom Jackson, the head of the race organizers, said. "It is a brown horse with one white stocking on the right foreleg. You registered 'Meadow Flier' yesterday upon your arrival with that description."

"But it's not the same animal," Comegys screeched. "Look! The white on the foreleg is some sort of paint or paste."

Comegys held up his hand, showing that some of the white pigment rubbed off on it. Tom Jackson came and felt the foreleg. When he stood up straight, his eye caught something else.

"There seems to be a similar material in a different color on the nose and chest of the horse," Jackson said, reaching out to feel both spots. "It looks as though this stuff is covering up a white area here and here."

Comegys' face fell when he heard this. Unable to hold himself back, he checked for himself. As he did, it was clear to him that Gallant Warrior was now standing in place of Mystic Mirror. What made it especially humorous to me was the Comegys could not state that he recognized the horse, or that he knew who was responsible for the switch.

"I still demand that you form a search party," Comegys yelled.

"We have a race to run in a few hours, Mr. Comegys," one of the locals said. "We'll be happy to organize a search when the race is complete, but no one would be willing to help you right now."

"Besides, if there was indeed a switch of animals," another said, "it happened in the middle of the night. We would never catch up to the thief—if there really is one. We would certainly not be back in time for the race."

"Will you still run the horse in the event?" Jackson asked.

"No, by the Seven Hells!" Comegys shouted. "This animal isn't even trained to jump a fence!"

"How would you know that, Mr. Comegys? Are you familiar with this horse?" Jackson asked pointedly.

"Of course not," Comegys backpedaled, realizing he had said too much. "It's just that he's clearly not a racehorse."

"But how would you know he can't jump fences?"

"I don't know," Comegys said. "I was just making a comment that it does not look like a racehorse."

"You sounded quite sure of it, Mr. Comegys. And from what I can see, this animal does not appear dissimilar to the others here in the barn," Jackson said. "He looks to be just as fit as the rest."

"I don't know this animal," Comegys protested. "There is no sense in entering a horse that isn't mine."

"Well, I'm afraid that we will not return your entry fee since you are withdrawing him so late."

"Someone stole my horse! And you want to punish me for that?" Comegys shrieked.

"There is something quite irregular about all this, Mr. Comegys," Jackson said. "Someone left a note for us, stating that you entered a registered horse under a false name in an event held earlier. If that turns out to be true, the Grand Chase will ban you from all future races."

"But—"

"The note also claimed that you cheated the bookies out of quite a bit of money," Jackson interrupted. "I hope that is not the case or the trouble you will face will be far more serious than any consequences the Grand Chase will levy. My advice to you, Mr. Comegys, will be to come clean with those you cheated, or you may not live to regret it."

"I'm the one whose horse was stolen, and you're accusing me of cheating?" Comegys shouted. "This is unheard of!"

"There is an easy way to see if you are telling the truth. Let's saddle this horse, and I'll take him out on the course to get him warmed up for the race."

"You'll do nothing of the sort," Comegys shouted. "I'm leaving. What has happened here is unfair and disgraceful. The Grand Chase will hear about this!"

Comegys ordered his groom to saddle the horse. The poor lad looked a bit green from the night before. He moved slowly—far too slowly for Comegys, who wanted to leave right away.

"Catch up to me on the road, boy," Comegys barked at him, then left.

Tom Jackson looked at the other two men who made up the race committee. They shrugged. Jackson shook his head and exited the barn.

11

The actual race was just as comical as I expected it to be. The boys riding the seven remaining horses were clearly still feeling the effects of their first exposure to whiskey. Two of them fell off—one when his horse refused a fence, the other when his mount landed awkwardly after a water obstacle. The other five looked like it was all they could do to hang on and stay in the saddle to the finish line.

It was the most raggedy-looking race I'd ever seen. Even the relatively unsophisticated crowd here in Allroyd knew something wasn't quite right. The two more favored horses finished out of the money, which caused more grumbling.

As at Whinage, I stayed to help clean up after the race. That afternoon, I listened to the three men in charge talking. Though they were unhappy with the state of the jockeys, they also saw the humor in it.

By noon the next day, I'd finished everything there was to do, including mucking out the stalls. Tom Jackson was still there. He came over to give me my pay.

"Ralph, I pride myself on being a good judge of men," he said. "There's too much intelligence behind your eyes for you to be a wandering laborer. And you weren't nearly as collywobbled as the others yesterday morning. I think you know exactly what happened with Comegys and his horse. Will you tell me?"

"Ah, Mr. Jackson," I said, scratching my head. "Hard tellin' not knowin'. I didn't see anything, you know that. From listening to what you had to say, though, it sounded to me like justice was done. Mr. Comegys didn't strike me as a good person. I'm sorry the race was so poorly ridden, but it will be one that everyone talks about for years, don't you think?"

"That it will, Ralph. That it will," he said, clapping me on the shoulder. "I don't expect I will see you again—at least, not as a wandering laborer."

"Well, I always hope to better myself, Mr. Jackson," I said.

His laughter followed me as I walked away, my bindle over my shoulder. I set off down the road to Jeffer's Ford. After spending the night sleeping outdoors, the next morning, Sir John's carriage appeared.

"Can we give you a lift, young man?" he asked.

"You might find me a bit whiffy to share your carriage, Sir John," I said. "Until I can get a bath, a shave, and a change of clothes, I'd better ride with your driver. I'll still smell just as awful, but I can make sure I'm downwind of him."

"Caz, I breed horses," he said. "If you smell like a barn, it won't put me off. Climb in."

I tossed my bindle up to the driver, who tucked it under the bench next to him. Then I climbed into the carriage. Sir John sniffed, then made sure all the flaps were pulled up so fresh air would circulate.

"You are a bit, as you say, 'whiffy,' but I can stand it if you can," he said. "Thank you for getting me the horse I paid for. Tell me what happened after Bill left."

"Bill?" I asked. "He called himself Dick Franklin."

"Majors and Minors!" Sir John snorted, laughing uproariously. "That's a good one. Dick Franklin works for me as well. He's… Let's just say that Dick is simple. About ten years ago, he wasn't paying attention to what he was doing, and put himself in the wrong place and got kicked in the head for it. He hasn't been the same since."

"So, if someone comes looking for Dick Franklin in relation to this incident, they'll be a bit disappointed," I remarked, chuckling.

"We are heading to Aquileia," Sir John said. "I will be communicating with the Grand Chase regarding Mr. Comegys and will share with them that I took measures to gain possession of Mystic Mirror. I will not be providing them with any specifics. In addition, I will be filing a case with the courts to cement my legal ownership."

"What about his claim that the markings on Gallant Warrior were as you described in your letter?" I asked.

"In the same letter, I also referred several times to the horse as the one which won the race at Polan," Sir John said. "Since Comegys disguised the horse with false markings, my reference to the one that won the event will take precedence."

"Did Dick—er, Bill—mention that Gallant Warrior isn't trained to jump?" I asked.

"What?"

"One of the things Comegys said when he recognized the horse as Gallant Warrior was that he knew the horse would not jump fences," I said. "That means the horse he sent to you could not have been the one which won at Polan."

"That makes my case even easier to prove," Sir John said with a smile. "All things considered, I would not want to be Samuel Comegys when the news of what he did spreads."

"His reputation will be ruined," I commented.

"That's not the worst of it," Sir John said. "The bookmakers will want their money back from Polan, and anywhere else he pulled the same trick. They are not nice people—especially to cheats."

We arrived in Aquileia nine days later on Freyday in the evening. Sir John promised he would deliver a bank draft to me on Maniday. I would take it to Pierre Luin and add it to my account.

That evening, as I dined at the Foaming Boar, I considered my circumstances. It was just six and a half months ago that I arrived in the city. In that time, I earned more than twenty thousand ducats. If Pierre Luin generated the returns he claimed, the income from my earnings plus the annuity from my grandfather would be enough to support myself indefinitely in the kind of style I hoped for.

I had no pressing need to work unless I wished to. That said, I was enjoying the different challenges that I'd taken on. I wondered who the next person would be who wanted my help and what the problem would be.

The next day was Njordday, one of Sally's days off. I went to Madam Saylor's house to call on her. Madam met me when I knocked at the rear entrance.

"Mr. FitzDuncan, please come in," she said.

"Thank you."

Madam Saylor headed for the front of her house. When she reached the parlor, she gestured for me to enter. She shut the door behind me.

"Please sit, Mr. FitzDuncan."

"Is Sally here?" I asked.

"I'm terribly sorry, Mr. FitzDuncan," she said. "Sally is not at home."

"I see. My apologies for disturbing you, madam," I said, beginning to rise.

"Mr. FitzDuncan, please sit," she said. "I would like to talk with you."

I lowered myself to the seat again. Madam Saylor took a chair nearby, positioned at a right angle to me. She leaned forward. I had the feeling I would not enjoy what she had to say.

"Mr. FitzDuncan, Sally is young, and unsophisticated," Madam Saylor began to explain. "She has a good enough head on her shoulders to realize that. You, despite the stigma of your surname, are clearly a gentleman in terms of upbringing and character. That is clear to anyone who has even the small amount of familiarity you and I have. I do not doubt your fondness for Sally, and I know she has enjoyed her outings with you. Even with that, do you see a future where you and Sally marry?"

"Madam Saylor, I have hardly even begun to get to know Sally," I protested. "The idea of marriage—"

"Mr. FitzDuncan, I will speak boldly and forthrightly," she said. "It would be a grave mistake for you or Sally to contemplate marriage. You keep company with rich men and titled nobility. Do you think Sally would ever be comfortable in your world?"

I wanted to protest, but as I struggled to form the words, I realized Madam Saylor was right. Though my friends were gracious and kind, Sally would never be their social equal. With Jenny, our time together was in the nature of scratching an itch we both felt. It was never a serious relationship. Things were different with Sally, and Madam Saylor's insight was on target. If my relationship with Sally went further, I would need to live in her world because she could not live in mine. That was not what I wanted.

"Mr. FitzDuncan, I'm sure you were hoping for something else today, but I'm equally certain you would never want to hurt Sally."

"You are correct on both counts, madam," I said.

"Please call me Phoebe," she said. "This is an intimate conversation and deserves to be conducted on first-name basis. May I call you Casimir?"

"My friends call me Caz," I said with a faint smile.

"Very well, Caz," she said, returning my smile. "I claim no gift of prophecy or second sight, but I foresee a bright future for you. Girls like Sally are fine for a bit of fun, but only if both of you understand that is all it will be—a bit of fun. I am not suggesting you adopt the life of a hermit. Just be aware that if one of these girls develops feelings for you, it will be better for you to break things off quickly."

"Mada—Phoebe," I said, catching myself, "I did not realize—"

"I didn't think so, Caz."

"I am not the most worldly-wise man. There has been little female influence in my life. They are a mystery to me."

"You are not alone in feeling that way," she said with a laugh.

I explained to her the unusual circumstances of my upbringing, and the dislike my stepmother displayed toward me. Then how I went to an all-male boarding school, followed by seven years in the Rangers. I confessed to Phoebe that it was only recently that I'd ever kissed a woman in a romantic way.

"You are operating at an even greater disadvantage to most men," she said. "Added to that is the problem of your unusual position in society. Your friend Lord Rawlinsford does not have the same issue. If he were to take up with a girl like Sally, she would know that it was only for a bit of slap and tickle. She would have no real expectation of becoming Lady Rawlinsford. Your lack of status allows someone like Sally to dream about something that is extremely unlikely to happen."

"Did you warn Sally away from me?" I asked.

"I did," she admitted, "when I realized what she was beginning to feel for you. If things continued, it would have become worse when Sally realized you were out of her reach. I understand if you are angry with me, but I hope, in time, you'll see why I did."

"No, Phoebe, I understand. I guess I am disappointed, though. While I was away, I was looking forward to seeing Sally again."

"I'm sure you're disappointed, but I predict that you will get over it in a few days. If things continued, it would have become worse," she said. "There would be no way for you to break it off without hurting Sally deeply, and I believe that you have no desire to cause her any pain."

"I do not," I said. "Your points are valid. I am in a difficult spot though."

"You are young, handsome, and well-mannered," she said with a grin. "You have discovered you enjoy female companionship and desire to gain even more experience."

"I do."

"This is incredibly forward of me," she said, "but I have a suggestion I would like to offer. I have never meddled in anyone's life like this before, but I believe this is an opportunity too good to let pass."

"What opportunity?"

"There is a woman I know. Like me, she is a widow. Her name is Celeste and her husband was Sir Abelard Nash. Though she is about ten years older than you, you would not know that to look at her. It difficult for a single woman of her age and station to enjoy any sort of a social life. I think it would do both of you some good if I were to introduce you," Phoebe said.

"Madam Saylor, I—"

"You need more experience with women," she interrupted, "particularly women of the class in which you are likely to marry one day. She misses male companionship. Having you as her escort opens many doors—socially—for both of you. You can learn a lot from her, and both of you will have fun. I've decided. Come to tea tomorrow afternoon. I will make sure Sally is not here in order to avoid any potential awkwardness."

"But—"

"Caz, you may protest all you like, but I am sure you will thank me later. It's just for tea, dear. I'm not asking you to sleep with her."

"Madam!" I protested.

"The two of you are on your own in that regard," Phoebe responded cheekily. "Just come for tea, Caz. If the two of you don't get along, I'll never bother you again."

I left Madam Saylor's after she extracted a promise from me to visit the next afternoon. While I walked, contrary thoughts chased themselves around in my head. I pondered her assessment of my unusual social status. Grudgingly, I admitted she was correct. A marriage to someone like Sally would be doomed. Unfortunately, marrying into the class to which my friends belonged would be a challenge because of my bastardy.

Countering that, fortunately, was my financial success in such a short time. I had almost enough money that I could support a wife in a moderate degree of comfort. If I somehow managed to earn as much again as what I had, I could maintain a family. The problem would be explaining to the father of a prospective bride how I obtained my money. What I'd done for Freddy, Pierre Luin, and Sir John could hardly be described as a career or a livelihood. The Gods alone knew when or if someone else might approach me with a challenge I might take on.

When I came out of my reverie, I found myself not far from Freddy's house. Deciding to follow through on what my unconscious mind decided for me, I went and knocked on the door. Roger answered.

"Mr. FitzDuncan here to see you, milord!" he hollered back.

"Send him back!" Freddy yelled in response.

Roger took my jacket and sword, hanging them up in the vestibule. I headed back to Freddy's sitting room. Freddy was sprawled on the sofa, still in his dressing gown, despite the fact that it was already late morning. He was massaging his temples.

"Welcome back, Caz," he said. "You didn't miss much while you were away. Pour us a glass of sherry while you're up."

"A little early, don't you think?" I asked.

"Hair of the dog that bit me last night," he said. "One glass, on top of the breakfast Roger just fed me, will set me to rights."

"A bit too much fun, then?" I asked as I poured a half a glass for each of us.

"If Linc Ellsworth ever suggests playing a drinking game," Freddy said, "don't."

"What sort of game?" I asked.

"I swear he was making up the rules as we went along," Freddy complained. "It had to do with one person shouting out a number, and then counting around either to the right or left depending on the number. You had two seconds to touch the tip of your nose with your finger if the count would land on you. If you didn't, you had to drink. And, if you touched your nose and the count would not have reached you, you had to drink. At least, that's what I think the rules were—something like that, anyway."

"I take it your command of sums was deficient," I commented.

"It wasn't that," Freddy said. "It was that the counting changed direction every time an odd number was called. Trying to figure out which direction the counting went the turn before took most of us more than two seconds. We argued a lot over the proper direction to count, and all of us got drunk as the Seven Hells—except Linc."

"Did you have fun?" I asked.

"Loads," Freddy admitted. "Then Ratty started singing."

"But Ratty can't sing a note," I said. "He couldn't carry a tune if you nailed it in a crate and strapped it to his back."

"I know," Freddy said with a chuckle, "but when he's drunk, he thinks he can. That makes it even funnier. Majors and Minors! I laughed so hard that my sides still hurt. How did things work out for Sir John?"

"Successfully," I said.

"And no one will come after you for being a horse thief?"

"That would be unlikely," I said, then shared with him the story of what happened at Allroyd.

12

"Stop, Caz. Stop," Freddy begged as I was recounting to him the progress of the race, describing to him the struggles of the boys in the saddle, still suffering the effects of their first time drinking whiskey. "My sides already hurt. I can't laugh any more or I'll break something. Let me get dressed, and I'll take you to the club for lunch."

Freddy came downstairs only a few minutes later. We walked to the Equestrian Club. On the way, Freddy amused me with more stories from the night before. The maître d' seated us in a quiet corner when we arrived.

"From the look on your face when you arrived at my house, I suspect you didn't come over to hear about our silliness last night. What's on your mind, Caz?" he asked.

I shared with him the gist of the conversation I had with Phoebe Saylor earlier that morning. Freddy listened attentively, nodding in spots. I finished by mentioning Phoebe's invitation to tea.

"She's right, you know," he said.

"I realized that on the way to your house," I admitted. "It puts me in a difficult position, though. And I am very uneasy about meeting Celeste Nash. It seems too contrived."

"No, Caz, Madam Saylor is right about that as well," Freddy said. "I don't know Celeste Nash well, but I know who she is. She's quite attractive—a redhead. Madam Saylor is correct in her assessment that girls like her maid are troublesome prospects. You are in a difficult position socially. You need a woman who is a second or third daughter."

"What does that have to do with anything?" I asked.

"We need to talk about a subject that I know makes you uncomfortable, Caz—your place in Aquileian society," Freddy said. "The circumstances of your birth put you in an unusual and uncomfortable position. Depending on the situation, you are either self-conscious about it, or defensive. I need you to try to set those feelings aside for a moment."

"Go on," I said guardedly.

"Regardless of who your mother was, your father is the Earl of the Eastern March. You were raised by your grandfather as though those duties would one day be yours—either to shoulder alone or to share. He sent you to school with the sons of the nobility and the wealthy, knowing that these are the people among whom you will live your life. At school, we learned that some of those who will inherit titles or riches are not gentlemen. You, despite your bastardy, are. You are a good man, Caz. The people who will matter in your life will see that clearly. I mean, look at who your friends are—Ratty, Linc, and me. Ratty's father owns one of the three largest trading companies in Aquileia. Linc's father is Count Bergin. Mine is a duke. We consider you a close friend."

"What does this have to do with what Madam Saylor said?" I asked.

"The woman you marry will need to be at ease in our company. That means she will come from the same sort of family. You are probably going to marry a girl whose father has a title, or controls substantial wealth," Freddy said.

"Freddy, my surname begins with 'Fitz.' What you're saying is ridiculous," I snorted.

"No, it's not," he stated firmly. "You know that marriages between families like mine are arranged for political or financial reasons. As the oldest son, I will not be free to marry whomever I wish. The union will need to be negotiated and approved by both families. That's not to say love will play no part. There are a number of young ladies whose families would be agreeable. I'm sure that within that group I will find someone," Freddy said.

"The reason I say you are eventually going to be looking for a younger daughter is that the obligation to use marriage to cement an alliance between families will not be a consideration for her. The second or third girl in a family typically gets no dowry," Freddy continued. "Her father is more concerned with getting her agreeably settled. That's where you come in. If you can provide your wife with a comfortable life, most fathers will overlook the fact that your surname begins with Fitz. There is one problem, though."

"Which is?"

"Your almost complete lack of experience with young ladies, particularly of the social background that should be your focus," Freddy said. "In addition, you are self-conscious, aware that the circumstances of your birth make you something 'other' in these circles. By now, you have seen that people like Linc, Ratty, and I don't care. There are more of us than there are of the kind who treated you so shabbily at school. Squiring the widow Nash around will give you the chance to see that and help you grow more comfortable moving in the social strata where you belong. Besides all that, I think you'll have fun."

"I'm glad you think so," I said with glum uncertainty.

"Oh, Caz," Freddy sighed. "C'mon, now. You will. Now, you need to think of a reason to see her again without Madam Saylor."

"Well, the Queen's Cup is only two weeks away," I said, referring to the season-ending steeplechase that was also a major social event.

"Too public," Freddy said. "Too much, too soon. If things go well between you two, there will be a time for you to appear together in that kind of setting, but probably not for a month or more."

"What about the theater?" I asked.

"Not for a first get-together," Freddy said. "You won't have the opportunity to have a conversation. I know! Invite her to go riding."

"I don't have a horse," I said.

"Borrow Oscar."

"Your horse?" I asked.

"Yes. We'll have Roger pack you a lunch again, and you take her to the lake, as you did with the other girl."

"Hardly original," I said.

"She won't know," Freddy countered. "And it provides ample opportunity for the two of you to talk and learn more about one another."

"Mr. Forteney, I believe I will ask for my weekly hot bath now," I said when I returned to my rooms later.

"Oh, Mr. Fitz, it's Njordday," he protested. "We're about to close the shop. I can't ask the lads to stay late to haul and heat the water."

"Lads?" You don't mind, do you? A demi-florin each for you," I said.

"Aye, Mr. Fitz," they both said cheerfully.

"Ah, Mr. Fitz, as your landlord, shouldn't that money come to me?" Forteney suggested.

"No," I said. "I've already paid my rent a year in advance—an amount that includes one hot bath each week. You've been well compensated, sir. The demi-florin is for the lads since I might be inconveniencing them late in the day on Njordday—unless you want to haul the water yourself?"

"Hardly," he snorted.

Lyle Forteney bantered like this every time I requested a bath. It was all in fun. The two boys he employed found our back-and-forth amusing.

My start to the next day was quite a bit later than usual. I slept with the windows open, and the night was unexpectedly chilly. The cool temperature and the warmth of my bed seduced me into rolling over and returning to slumber's grasp instead of starting my day when I first woke.

I dressed in one of my "Baron Winstonworth" suits and went to the Foaming Boar for lunch. When I returned, I went down to the book shop and browsed the titles of the used books. Forteney had given me permission to read any of the used books he had on hand. I selected a book on the history of Aquileia and returned upstairs to read.

At the appropriate hour, I put the book down and left. Walking to Madam Saylor's, I felt uncomfortable. Yes, Freddy said I would have fun, but I felt more like I was going to be shown how unsuitable I was.

Phoebe Saylor opened the door and ushered me inside. In her parlor was a woman who was strikingly attractive. I won't say "beautiful" because her features were a bit too strong, but she was damned desirable—to my eyes, at least. As Freddy said, her hair was red, but not the carroty type. Her hair was much deeper and darker in color. The skin of her face was not the pale shade I had seen with most redheads. Hers showed some color, along with the expected freckles. Clearly, Celeste Nash spent time out of doors. I knew she was ten years older than I was, but she did not look it.

Phoebe introduced us. I bowed over the widow Nash's hand when she offered it to me. All the lessons my grandfather taught me as a boy about proper deportment were swirling in my head.

Phoebe instructed me to sit while she poured tea. I sat up straight, on the forward half of a chair, with my knees and feet together as I was taught long ago. Phoebe's fussing with the teapot and cups was a welcome distraction for my eyes, and preventing me from staring at Celeste Nash.

After Phoebe served the tea, she sat down. There was a brief period of awkward silence. Then Phoebe explained why she invited us to meet.

My face must have been an interesting shade of scarlet while Phoebe was talking about me. I was as embarrassed as I think I have ever been. Celeste listened and examined me with appraising eyes.

"For you, Celeste, Caz provides you with the opportunity to resume a more active social life without the awkwardness and vulnerability of being a widow," Phoebe said. "You've complained to me several times how difficult it has been. Having Caz escort you removes the stigma of being unattached and gets you back in circulation."

"Hmm," Celeste murmured.

"I'm not proposing an arrangement that lasts forever," Phoebe declared. "Just for the time being, when you both benefit. You will know when it has run its course, and I'm sure you will part friends."

"Madam," I said, addressing Celeste, "despite my very great discomfort right now, I believe Phoebe would not have suggested this without confidence that we would both gain from the experience. May I offer a suggestion?"

"Please," Celeste said.

"I understand through a mutual acquaintance that you are fond of riding," I said. "The weather promises fair for tomorrow. May I call on you tomorrow? We can ride to the lake. I will provide lunch, and we can talk. Perhaps we will discover that Phoebe's idea is unworkable. Perhaps we will find each other interesting enough to meet again."

"I would enjoy a nice ride like that," Celeste said. "All too soon, the weather will turn, and there won't be opportunities. Yes, you may call on me. At what hour?"

"Is ten o'clock acceptable?" I asked.

She nodded.

The following morning dawned bright and clear. I invited myself to Freddy's for breakfast. That provided him the chance to quiz me regarding the tea the previous day. He grew very excited when I told him I would be taking the widow Nash out for a ride later that morning. He hurried to dress after we ate and instructed Roger to prepare a lunch that could be carried in saddle bags.

"Stay right here, Caz," he said. "I'll go to the club and retrieve Oscar."

I was beginning to be concerned about the hour when Freddy reappeared on Oscar—a handsome dun gelding. He slid from the saddle and grabbed the saddlebags. Roger was ready when Freddy brought them into the kitchen and packed them with whatever he prepared. I did see a bottle of wine and two wine glasses Roger wrapped in a blanket.

"Have a wonderful day," Freddy said as he fastened the saddle bags.

"I hope to," I said. "In any event, I'll be able to tell you when I bring Oscar back."

"I'm already looking forward to it," he said.

The Gods must have been smiling upon me. We could not have asked for better weather. It was one of those marvelous days in late Twiman that remind you of the summer past, only without oppressive heat.

When I arrived at Celeste's house, a clock nearby was chiming ten. She was already mounted and waiting. Her hair was up, but she wore no hat. That explained the color of her complexion, I realized.

'I like a man who is prompt," she said. "Shall we?"

"Let's," I replied.

As we picked our way through the streets of the city, I noted that she sat the saddle with graceful ease. Clearly, she was an experienced rider. We did not talk as we rode.

Shortly after we passed through the west gate of the city, Celeste clicked her tongue, and her horse began to canter. Oscar responded without anything more than a nudge from my knees, and we drew even with her. As soon as we did, Celeste looked over with a grin. Her horse broke into a gallop, and I could hear Celeste laughing. Oscar charged forward in response to my instruction.

It was not until we were almost at the park that Oscar and I managed to catch Celeste. When we did, she reined in, slowing to a walk. Her face was flushed with exertion and excitement, and strands of her hair framed her face where they escaped.

"It's too nice a day to merely plod along," she explained. "And Sheila likes a bit of a run. I hope you didn't mind."

"Not at all," I said. "It has been months since I last rode. I just realized how much I missed it."

"You don't own a horse?" she asked incredulously.

"I do not," I admitted. "Oscar here belongs to a good friend."

"If I may be so bold," she began, "why don't you own a horse?"

"It's not because I don't like them," I said. "In fact, it's probably the opposite. And that's the biggest reason I do not own one right now."

"Explain," she said.

"If I owned a horse, I would feel obligated to spend time with him or her every day. Otherwise, it's not fair to the animal. There is a bond that must be nurtured and maintained," I said. "Right now, after seven years in the Rangers and four years at school before that, I am enjoying my freedom—the freedom to do as I please, even if that means doing nothing."

"I do try to spend time with Sheila," she said. "She helped keep me sane the last year. But, still, don't you need a horse?"

"Not at present," I said.

"You know, Phoebe didn't say exactly what you do for a living, Mr. FitzDuncan," Celeste said.

'That might be a conversation better conducted while we have lunch," I suggested.

By now, we were within sight of the lake. I took the lead and headed Oscar in the direction I wanted to go. There was a nice shady spot with a good view I discovered on my previous visit.

When we reached the place I had in mind, I reined Oscar in and dismounted. I offered my hand to Celeste, but she shook her head. I then proceeded to unpack what Roger prepared for us. After spreading out the blanket, I set the food out, uncorked the bottle of wine, and poured us each a glass.

"Now that we are comfortable, Mr. FitzDuncan—"

"Please call me Caz," I requested. "If we are going to be friends, we should start that way."

"We may become good friends," she replied, "but allow me to judge our progress, Mr. FitzDuncan."

I nodded, feeling chastened.

"Now, how do you make your living, Mr. Fitz?" she asked.

"I suppose the easiest way to describe it," I said, "is that I help people."

"Help them do what?"

"Recover things that have been taken, I suppose," I said.

"You suppose?"

"It is difficult for me to know how much to share," I said. "Each of the circumstances has been different, and all of them have been sensitive in nature. I don't want to violate the confidence of the people I have helped."

"Can you describe in vague terms what you've done?" she asked.

Without names or much in the way of details, I did. It sounded rather simple the way I described it. Fortunately, Celeste was clever enough to understand that, judging by the questions she asked.

"And you can make a living doing this?" she asked.

"Yes," I said. "It would be unseemly for me to share, but it has been financially rewarding. Now, if you don't mind, would you please tell me about you, Madam Nash?"

"My father owns a successful textile manufactory," she said. "I was raised with every advantage. Eighteen years ago, Sir Abelard Nash saw me riding, learned who I was, and asked my father if he could court me. We fell in love and married just over seventeen years ago, on the summer solstice. Sir Abelard was quite a bit older. He died two and a half years ago. The doctor said his heart gave out."

"I'm sorry for your loss," I said sincerely.

"I'm almost accustomed to his absence," she said. "I no longer miss him so terribly. But I find that the social life of a single woman of my age is limited. At the few gatherings where I am welcome, I attract attention from men who are more interested in the size of the estate Sir Abelard left me than in providing meaningful companionship."

"Really?" I asked unguardedly.

"I don't find it a laughing matter, Mr. FitzDuncan," she said sternly.

"Madam," I protested. "I did not mean to doubt your word. At the risk of compounding my gaffe, let me just say that I think you are extremely attractive. I cannot imagine being more interested in your money than the pleasure of your company."

"And now I begin to understand why Phoebe introduced us," Celeste said with a laugh. "That is rather forward of you, Caz. I shall forgive you if you explain why you find me attractive."

"Your physical attractiveness is compelling," I said hesitantly. "But more appealing to me was the joy I saw on your face as we rode. You ride well, and clearly enjoy the exercise. More than that, I sensed you revel in the feeling of freedom you have in the saddle."

The slow smile Celeste gave me told me that, however inept my phrasing may have been, she liked what I said. We spent the rest of our afternoon pleasantly, talking about nothing and everything. After we arrived back at her house, she allowed me to kiss her cheek.

"May I call on you again, Madam?" I asked.

"I shall be disappointed if you do not," she replied with a smile.

13

Thus began my relationship with Celeste. Things moved at a slow pace—far more slowly than with Jenny or Sally. Celeste explained that I should expect that in any future romantic entanglements.

She allowed me to escort her to various events. Along the way, Celeste counseled me in the finer points of manners that my grandfather had overlooked and in how to woo a woman of more suitable social status. Linc Ellsworth's holiday gala just before the winter solstice was a high point.

For the first time, I was thankful for my grandfather insisting I learn basic dance steps. When I was a boy, he drafted different armsmen to serve as my partners while he kept time by clapping his hands and calling out our missteps. I dreaded these lessons and I knew the armsmen did as well.

Nonetheless, that evening, I knew all the steps to the Basse, the Quadrille, the Black Alman, and even the Rufty Tufty. Both of us found ourselves in demand as dance partners for others. After the party, Celeste invited me to share her bed for the first time, and so began another aspect of my education.

We spent the night together more often than not during the cold winter months. As we neared the end of the month of Goa, I invited Celeste to dinner. The excuse was the anniversary of my arrival in the city.

The dinner ended more somberly than I anticipated. After we finished eating, Celeste reached across the table and clasped my hands. The sad smile on her face was not what I expecting to see.

"Caz, I'm afraid our time together has reached its end," she said.

"What?" I choked out past the sudden lump in my throat.

"Do you remember meeting Sir Thornton Mellon at the holiday party?" she asked.

"Vaguely," I replied, remembering a man who seemed to be roughly fifty years old.

"He just returned to the city and came to call upon me," she said. "We have spent some time together, and he is interested in pursuing a relationship with me. It appears to show some promise."

"I understand," I said after having the opportunity to absorb what she was saying.

"You have learned what you needed from me," she said. "And though I am genuinely quite fond of you, what we have is not love. I'm sure you are disappointed, but I hope you are not heartbroken."

"I suppose I always knew our time together would reach an end, Celeste," I said with a gravelly voice. "I would never want to stand in the way of your happiness."

I escorted Celeste home. At her doorstep, she offered me her cheek. I kissed it gently, waited for her to step inside, then trudged back to my rooms.

She was correct. Though we had been lovers, we were not in love. I was sad because I enjoyed her company and knew I would miss her.

By the time I crawled into bed, my overall feeling was one of wistful gratitude. I learned many important subtleties from Celeste. My memories of our time together would always be happy ones.

I did not have a long time to wallow in self-pity. Two days later when I paid my rent for the upcoming year, Lyle Forteney told me someone was looking for me when I returned from exercising at my salle. The man, Kirk Johanson, left a card and told Lyle he would return in the afternoon.

Just after the clock in the market square outside rang one there was a knock on my door. I went to open it. Standing there was a short, slight man with a mustache. He appeared to be somewhere in his forties, judging by the gray at his temples.

"Kirk Johanson?" I asked.

"Yes. Casimir FitzDuncan?"

"Please come in," I offered, standing aside. "Have a seat. I apologize. I don't entertain often and have no refreshments to offer you."

"This is not a social call, Mr. FitzDuncan," Johanson said with a smile. "Pierre Luin recommended I seek you out. I have a problem, and he believes you can help me."

"I hope I can," I replied as I sat facing him. "What is the problem?"

"My stepfather, Dale Cameron," he said. "He refuses to surrender my mother's jewelry to me. The pieces are family heirlooms. He has no legal right to them. When my father died, he specifically mentioned in his will that the pieces were to come to me upon my mother's death."

"What is his excuse for not surrendering the pieces?" I asked.

"He claims my mother sold them because she needed the money," Johanson said. "That is a lie. I provided my mother with a healthy allowance even after she married Cameron. That leech did not contribute anything. Nevertheless, I made sure my mother was comfortable."

"I take it you are a man of means," I commented.

"I own three iron furnaces upriver," he said.

"Ah," I said.

I didn't know much about the iron industry, but I knew that the ore needed to be smelted to remove impurities. Smelting took place in furnaces. They were typically located near rivers since they used waterwheels to power bellows, which helped them increase output. Using the river to transport both ore and the smelted iron was also advantageous. Owning three such furnaces probably made Johanson a fairly important figure in the industry.

"Do you think this Cameron has sold the pieces yet?" I asked.

"I don't believe so," he said. "He has not had time. We just buried my mother last week."

"I'm sorry for your loss," I said.

"Thank you."

"And you asked Cameron for the jewelry and he claimed it was sold. Were there any witnesses to this discussion?"

"Yes, my mother's solicitor," Johanson said. "We gathered a few days ago for the reading of her will. She left the house and whatever was in her bank account to Cameron."

"Where do you think the jewelry is?" I asked.

"Somewhere in the house."

"Did you ask if you could look for it?"

"I did. He refused, saying that it was his house now and he would not allow me in to look for something that she sold years before," Johanson said.

"Did you ask your solicitor about suing Cameron to get the jewelry back?" I inquired.

"I did. The problem is that a lawsuit will take time," Johanson explained. "In that time, Cameron will find a way to sell the jewelry."

"So, you need someone to go through the house and find the jewelry if it is there, and steal it back."

"That's correct."

"And you said Pierre Luin referred you to me," I said. "Did he share with you what my terms are?"

"Yes," Johanson confirmed. "You get half the value of what you recover."

"How much is this jewelry worth?" I asked.

"Conservatively speaking, thirty thousand ducats," Johanson said. "I'm willing to pay you half that amount if you can retrieve it. The money is secondary to me. These pieces have been in the family for generations."

"Before I take this on, I would like to have some confirmation of what was in your father's will," I stated.

"I understand. We can pay a visit to my solicitor," he said.

We decided to do that immediately. Johanson paid for a hackney. We arrived at his solicitor's office in minutes.

The lawyer showed me the will, and it clearly stated that the jewelry would pass to Kirk upon his mother's death. That removed any qualms I had about helping the man. The only questions that remained were regarding the feasibility.

"Does your stepfather leave the house?" I asked.

"Not often," Johanson said.

"Can you think of a way of getting him out, even for a brief time?"

"I can contrive a reason," the solicitor said. "If I send him a note asking him to come to the office regarding access to his late wife's account, he will come. We still have not filed the papers with the bank."

"How much is in her account?" I asked.

"Over two thousand ducats," the solicitor replied. "Plenty enough to garner his interest."

"Who will be in the house when he departs?"

"Only the housekeeper," Johanson said. "If we arrange this for Freyday, she goes to market around ten o'clock."

"Let's do that," I said.

"How much space does the jewelry take up?" I asked.

"My mother kept it in an enameled box about this big," Johanson said, indicating with his hands.

"Roughly eight inches by twelve inches and less than two inches thick?" I asked.

"That's about right."

When we left the solicitor's office, I asked Johanson to show me the house. It was in the same part of the city as Freddy's, so I was familiar with the area. After Johanson had the hackney deliver me to the bookseller's, I returned on foot to examine the property more closely.

Like many of the neighborhoods in this section of the city, the houses were close to one another. They fronted a street. Between them and their neighbors to the rear was a narrow service alley.

In the service alley there was enough vegetation that I could conceal myself while waiting for the housekeeper to depart. When she did, I would enter the house and look for the jewelry.

Two days later was Freyday. I positioned myself in the front of the house first. Johanson's solicitor asked Cameron to come to his office at ten. When I saw Cameron leave, I moved to a spot in the service alley where I could wait for the housekeeper to depart.

I was starting to wonder if she already left while I was on the other side of the house. A nearby clock indicated the quarter hour a few minutes before. I was just about to give up my watch and approach the rear entrance when she appeared.

She was an older woman and did not move quickly. I heard the clock ring the half hour before she disappeared at the other end of the alley. With one last check to see if anyone was outside looking, I went to the door and let myself in.

Once inside, I went upstairs immediately. I entered what must be the master bedroom, and quickly went to work. The first place I checked was under the bed, feeling for a loose floorboard. There wasn't one.

Then I began to go through the drawers. Since I was searching for an object of some size, I did not feel the need to dump the contents on the floor. I could stick my hand in and sweep around, feeling for the jewelry box.

My search of the drawers yielded nothing. I then searched the armoires. They, too, did not hold the box. I even felt under the mattress of the bed—no luck.

There were three other rooms on this floor. One was clearly the housekeeper's. I ignored that. Another was a guest room. The third looked like a study, with a desk and a low sideboard.

I searched the desk carefully, drawer by drawer. There was nothing of note in it. On my hands and knees, I started going through the sideboard. Behind a stack of papers, I finally found the jewelry box. Pulling it out, I opened it quickly to make sure it was not empty. Unfortunately, as I looked inside, I heard the front door of the house shut.

As quickly as I could, I moved everything back close to the way I found it. I shut the door of the sideboard and considered how I would escape. The housekeeper's room was in the rear of the house. I could open the window and climb out. Once outside, I hoped the first-floor window had enough of an upper sill that I could put my feet on it while I considered how to get down the rest of the way.

I tip-toed out of the study into the housekeeper's room. As quietly as possible, I shut the door behind me. I tucked the jewelry box into my shirt and opened the window.

Looking out, I did not see any alternative methods of escape other than lowering myself from the window and dropping the rest of the way. There were, at least, some bushes below to break my fall. I slid my legs out and lowered myself down. When I was fully extended, I let go.

Sadly, the bushes underneath me were as thorny as the Seven Hells. My legs, arms, and even my face were scratched to the point of bleeding. Cursing silently, I picked myself up and headed down the alley, making my way toward my rooms.

"Stop thief!" came from behind me before I reached the cross street, as Cameron discovered his loss.

He must have seen me drop from the second floor and run up to check. I picked up my pace. When I reached the cross street, I turned left and was almost bowled over by a member of the City Watch, hurrying to respond to Cameron's shouts.

"What's all this then," he demanded after seeing my bloody scratches and having felt the jewelry box under my shirt. "Hands on your head!"

"This is not what it looks like," I said, "though I am aware that what you see looks pretty bad. You probably have no choice except to arrest me. If I may beg one favor from you, I ask only one thing. Whatever you do, do not give this box back to the man who is shouting. The box does not belong to him any more than it does to me. Turn it over to Sir Oliver West, as it will be important evidence."

"You'll come peaceful like?" he asked.

"I will," I said. "If you let me unbuckle my sword, I'll hand it over to you."

"I'll unbuckle it, if you don't mind," he said.

"Of course," I agreed.

"Good job, you," came a voice from behind me. "This thief took something from me. I want it back immediately."

"Terribly sorry, sir," the watchman said. "It's important evidence that a crime has been committed. If I hand it over, this miscreant will go free."

"That's fine," Cameron said. "I'm not interested in pressing charges. Just give me what he took."

"Terribly sorry, sir, but I can't do that. It's not up to you whether this man goes to trial. That's for the magistrates to decide. Until then, this here box is evidence and I must take it to the Palace of Justice."

"That's preposterous," Cameron said angrily. "I demand that you give me back the box he took!"

"Sir, I explained why I cannot," the watchman said sternly. "It is not a matter for argument."

Cameron then did something foolish. He tried to grab the box the watchman was holding. The watchman snatched it out of his reach.

"Do that again, sir, and I will arrest you for interfering with official business."

"But it's mine," Cameron whined.

"It is evidence," the watchman replied sternly. "If it is indeed yours, the court will return it to you. Based on your behavior, though, I am beginning to doubt the strength of your claim."

The watchman escorted me to the Palace of Justice. He asked for and received my promise of good behavior, so he did not put manacles on me. After we were sure Cameron was not following us, he asked me to explain.

"It's a bit complicated, sir," I said. "A matter for lawyers and a magistrate to decide. That's why I ask you to hand the box over to Sir Oliver."

"If it involves lawyers, he's welcome to it," the watchman said with a chuckle. "Can't stand 'em, myself."

When we arrived at the Palace of Justice, his colleagues took me and led me to a cell. I would say they threw me in, but their actions, while plenty rough, fell just short of that. The cell was disgusting.

Though it was midday, the entire level the cell was on was dim and smelled of mildew. They shoved me into the cell hard enough that I stumbled. When I put my hand on the floor to steady myself, it felt disgustingly slick. There was no furniture except for two buckets. One held a ladle. The other did not. I figured out what each was for from that. I decided instantly that I would remain standing until Sir Oliver came for me.

Unfortunately, that was several hours. To lessen the discomfort of standing on the stone floor, I began to pace. I must have traversed the cell hundreds of times when Sir Oliver finally appeared.

"Well, Mr. FitzDuncan," he said through the small grate in the door. "I had a feeling I would see you again, and in this very spot."

Hello, Sir Oliver," I replied. "Would you be so kind as to let me out, and I will explain?"

"I'm not feeling very kindly toward you at the moment, Mr. FitzDuncan," Sir Oliver said. "I've just spent a very unpleasant time with a Mr. Dale Cameron and his lawyer. Did you know I despise lawyers, Mr. FitzDuncan?"

"I did not," I answered, "though in your position, I imagine it would be easy to cultivate a healthy dislike for them."

"I am also loath to release someone who was quite clearly engaged in an act of robbery not long before being apprehended by one of my men."

"Sir Oliver, I will not waste your time by trying to deny it," I said. "In this case, however, my actions put me on the side of the Gods and all the heavenly beings. I hope you did not return the jewelry box to Cameron."

"I did not," he said. "Now I want you to explain why I was correct not to do so. If you don't, you may be staying here for quite some length of time."

"The jewels are family heirlooms and belong to Kirk Johanson, under the terms of his late father's will," I said. "Dale Cameron was Johanson's stepfather. On the recent death of Johanson's mother, Cameron refused to surrender the jewels."

"You saw the father's will?" Sir Oliver asked.

"I insisted upon it," I stated firmly.

"Very well," Sir Oliver sighed.

A moment later, the door of my cell opened.

14

Sir Oliver allowed me to leave. He did not give me the jewelry box. Kirk Johanson needed to bring his father's will in order to get them. He did that later that day.

Before that happened, I had an interesting conversation with Lyle Forteney. It started when I returned the book on history that I borrowed from the shop. I was actually on my way to snatch a free breakfast from Freddy.

"Ah, Mr. FitzDuncan," he said. "Just the man I wanted to see."

"What's wrong?" I asked.

"Nothing is wrong," he said. "I just wanted to alert you that when your rent comes due next year, you will probably be paying it to someone else."

"Really? Are you planning on selling the building?" I asked.

"The building and the business," he said. "A gentleman offered me twelve thousand for the building."

"And the business?" I asked.

"He doesn't want the business."

"Lyle, I know this might seem hard to believe, but I might be interested," I said.

"In the building?"

"In purchasing both, but only if you agree to stay on to run the bookshop for a period of several years," I said. "Before we proceed further, I will need to ask some sensitive questions."

"Like how much money the business earns?"

"Exactly," I said.

"Between four and five hundred ducats a year after the taxes are paid," he said.

"What if I offered to buy the building and the business for fifteen thousand, keep you on to run the bookshop, and pay you a salary to do so?" I inquired.

"You have that kind of cash?" Lyle asked. "Please pardon my incredulity, but you arrived a year ago with, well, not much."

"This has been a successful year," I said with a shrug.

"Again, please pardon me, Mr. Fitz, but you don't seem to have a job," he said. "Is what you are doing legal?"

"Mostly," I joked.

"It's not criminal, Lyle," I said quickly, noting his troubled expression. "Sir Oliver West and I parted on good terms yesterday. What I do requires a rather lengthy explanation. I promise to provide it, if you'll allow my finance manager to look at your books."

"You have a person to manage your finances?"

"I do."

"And what you're doing is not criminal?" he asked.

"Again, Lyle, I promise the full explanation, but I don't feel it's criminal," I said.

"Sure," Lyle said. "Send him over. He can examine the ledgers. If it all works out, what you're offering is better than the other gentleman. I would like to keep running the business. Being able to reap the benefits of the sale and still do what I love would be ideal."

"His name is Pierre Luin," I said. "I will have him come by. Do you need to give the other man an answer soon?"

"I told him I needed a few days to think it over," Lyle said.

"Good. I'll have Pierre come see you."

With an extra spring in my step, I left and headed for Freddy's house. I hoped Pierre would agree that this was a worthwhile investment. Quite frankly, the thing that attracted me most was the building. Pierre explained it to me in an early meeting.

"The one thing that Gods aren't making more of is land," he said. "Owning property, particularly here in the capital, is one of the most solid investments you can make."

The shop was on a market square that drew decent traffic, to my amateur eye. It was clearly a profitable business, or Lyle would not have agreed so readily to allow Pierre to examine the books. While I did not expect it to generate the returns my other investments with Pierre were earning, I would secure living quarters for the rest of my life.

When I knocked on Freddy's door, Roger answered. Unusually, his face bore a concerned look. He hesitated once, then twice before calling out my presence to Freddy.

"Oh, Seven Hells!" I heard Freddy say, then heard more muttering from inside.

"Caz, sorry, my friend, not today," Freddy shouted.

I nodded to Roger and turned away. Freddy clearly had an overnight guest he did not want me to meet. With a smile on my face, I wondered who it was.

I headed to Pierre's office, stopping by a bakery on the way to grab a bite to eat. As I gnawed away a hunk of lemon bread, I pondered why Freddy did not want me to meet his visitor. He'd never been bashful about my knowing of his dalliances with girls like Jenny. That indicated to me that the girl in the house just now was someone of higher social standing—someone who might be a possible marriage prospect. It might also be someone I knew, which would have made the encounter even more uncomfortable. Then again, he was probably just protecting the woman's modesty—as a gentleman should.

When I arrived at Pierre's office, he heard the outer door open and called for me to wait in the vestibule. A few minutes later, he accompanied a man to the door. Seeing me, he put his hand on the man's shoulder to stop him.

"How fortuitous!" Pierre said. "The very man I wanted you to meet. Barclay Stone, this is Casimir FitzDuncan. Mr. FitzDuncan, Mr. Stone has a problem in which you might be able to provide assistance."

"My business with Pierre will only take a moment, Mr. Stone," I said as we shook hands. "If you don't mind waiting briefly—"

"That would be fine, Mr. FitzDuncan," he replied.

Entering Pierre's office, I did not even bother to sit down. I explained the content of my discussion with Lyle Forteney. As I did, Pierre raised his eyebrows.

"We will need to see how profitable the business is," he said, "but the chance to buy the building is the more important part. It will be a solid investment. It might not generate as much income as some of the things I have your money in now, but it will appreciate in value over time."

"Mr. Forteney knows you will be coming at some point," I said. "Whenever it fits into your schedule will be fine."

"I should be free enough this afternoon to stop by," Pierre said. "It's an interesting coincidence, you stopping by right now. Mr. Stone and I were discussing a real estate investment that did not turn out well for him. That is what he wishes to discuss with you."

"I hope I can be of assistance," I said.

"That is my hope as well."

Mr. Stone was waiting in the vestibule, and we left together. He looked around cautiously. Satisfied no one was close enough to overhear, he stopped me with his hand on my arm.

"I was just cheated out of six thousand ducats," he said. "Pierre tells me you might be able to help me get it back."

"I'll need to know more," I said, "before I can determine whether I can help you. Did Pierre explain my usual terms?"

"He did. You keep half of what you recover," Stone said. "That does not bother me. It's the principle of the thing that irks me. I can't stand the thought that this scoundrel might get away with it."

"Tell me what happened," I asked.

"Just over a month ago, I was having dinner at the Piebald Pony," Stone said as he resumed walking. "The man at the next table was lamenting to an acquaintance of mine that he had suffered a setback. From what I overheard, I gathered he was a 'name' for Perkins."

"Perkins?" I asked. "The insurers?"

"Yes."

"What does being a 'name' mean?" I inquired. "I've heard the expression, but I don't understand it."

"Before a company, such as Hawkins Trading, sets sail with a cargo, they purchase insurance from, well, Perkins is the largest such provider in the kingdom," Stone explained. "Perkins as an entity doesn't really have anything in the way of assets. It helps if you think of them as bookmakers."

"Bookmakers? As in, betting?" I asked.

"Yes," Stone said. "Now, before the ship sets sail, Hawkins Trading bets a certain amount of money that the ship will sink or some other misfortune will happen."

"Even though they don't want that to occur?" I said, slightly puzzled.

"Yes. Even though they hope it doesn't happen," Stone continued. "Perkins then informs its members, the 'names,' about the cargo and its value, the destination, and the shipping company. The 'name,' with Perkins's guidance, then determines the amount Hawkins will need to pay, or, to continue my earlier analogy, bet. The 'name' is, therefore, betting that nothing bad will happen to the cargo, for if it does, he must pay Hawkins for the declared value of it. Most of the time, the cargo is delivered without incident, and the 'name' keeps the amount that Hawkins 'bet' because he won and Hawkins lost. Perkins keeps a small percentage for facilitating the transaction."

"It sounds risky," I commented.

"It can be," Stone agreed. "On the other hand, it's possible to earn substantial amounts of money if you manage to avoid losses. To get back to my story, from what I overheard, this man was acting as though he was a 'name' for Perkins. He was using the name 'Lars Levere.' A ship he insured was captured by Rhetian pirates on the way back from Nagah on the southern continent. Levere now needed to pay Coombs Trading for the declared value of the cargo, which he said was six thousand ducats. He was lamenting the fact that his assets were not liquid. He needed cash and needed it quickly."

"Uh-oh," I said, sensing where this tale was heading.

"Uh-oh, indeed," Stone said with a chagrined smile. "My acquaintance asked Levere what assets he had that he could sell. The man replied that the most convenient thing would be for him to mortgage a piece of property he owned, but the banks would take at least thirty days before they would issue him the funds, and he needed the money right away. It was at this point that my greed started to betray my better judgment."

"I'm going to guess that the property he was discussing was worth significantly more than the six thousand he needed and that he promised to pay you generously for lending him the money," I said.

"Quite so," Stone said. "The property was supposedly one of the two vacant lots on Elmir Avenue."

Elmir Avenue is near Freddy's house in an affluent neighborhood. In the older, established neighborhoods of the city, there were not many empty pieces of land. A lot like that would easily be worth near to ten thousand ducats.

"Levere seemed trustworthy," Stone said, shaking his head in dismay. "He certainly looked and behaved like someone who would be a 'name' for Perkins. When we met the next afternoon, he insisted we go to a solicitor to draw up the agreement."

"His solicitor?" I asked.

"We went to the offices of Dewey and Howe," Stone said. "They are not the firm I use, but—"

"I've heard of them," I said.

"Exactly. They're respected. Because he was pressed for time, he said that Gordon Howe agreed to stay late in the office to accommodate us," Stone explained. "He asked if I could obtain a bank draft for six thousand and meet him there at six o'clock, after which he would take me to dinner. In the meantime, he needed to go to Perkins to inform them that he would be able to satisfy his obligation in the morning after the banks opened."

"Please continue, Mr. Stone," I said. "This is fascinating. I thought I knew what was coming next but Dewey and Howe being involved was something I did not expect."

"Oh, they weren't," Stone said. "But I did not realize that until later."

I gestured for him to resume his narrative.

"When I arrived at the office, a distinguished gentleman opened the door and introduced himself as Gordon Howe," Stone said. "Levere was already waiting. A mortgage document was already prepared. I scanned it quickly, and it seemed legitimate to me. Levere then asked if I wanted the deed to the property or if I would be willing to allow Dewey and Howe to hold it in escrow. It seemed safer to allow the lawyers to have it so I agreed to their suggestion. I surrendered the bank draft, and we went to dinner, where we toasted our mutual success. That was the last I saw of either one of them."

I could not help but laugh at this point. When I saw the expression on Barclay Stone's face, I reined in my amusement. No one likes to be fooled so badly.

"I'll guess that when you asked your acquaintance about Levere, he told you he only met him the night you overheard him," I noted.

"Yes."

"When you went to try to find this Levere, no one at Perkins ever heard of him," I suggested.

"Correct."

"And when you went to Dewey and Howe, you discovered there was no one named Gordon Howe with the firm."

"Also correct."

"How long after that last dinner did you wait before beginning your search?" I inquired.

"A month."

"Majors and Minors, man!" I exclaimed. "They could be anywhere by now!"

"Except they're not," Stone said. "Two days ago, I saw the man who called himself Gordon Howe. I followed him as discreetly as I could. I can show you the house he went to."

"Really?" I asked. "That will be helpful. Can you find your way there again?"

"Of course," he said.

"If you have the time, let's take a hackney, and you can show me," I said. "We can draw the shades to prevent anyone from seeing us."

"Taking my money back from these criminals is my highest priority," he said. "I'm happy to give you half if it means they do not profit from my stupidity."

"I wouldn't say you were stupid, Mr. Stone," I said. "A bit incautious, yes. But meeting you in the office of Dewey and Howe was a clever play on their part. I wonder how they managed it?"

"I learned that Dewey and Howe closes at half past four every day," Stone said. "The only time they meet with a client after those hours would be at the client's residence or office."

"Ah!" I said.

When we reached the market square near my rooms, we hailed a hackney. Stone gave the driver directions, and we headed north and west. We reached what I would classify as a "workingman's neighborhood."

The houses were small, with no space between one and the next. There was no distance between the front of the house and the street. These were the homes of the tradesmen who kept the city of Aquileia running. I would not be surprised to find Lyle Forteney living in a neighborhood like this.

"Seven Hells!" Stone hissed as he peered out the window. "That's Levere!"

He started to move as though he wanted to climb out of the hackney and confront the man right there. Instead, I shoved Stone away from the window so he would not be seen and held my finger to my lips, indicating he should keep quiet. Then I looked at the man he indicated. He was not dressed as nicely as when Stone encountered him previously. His clothes were ordinary—not much different from what I normally wore. I watched as he went in the front door of a house.

"Is that the place?" I asked Stone.

"Yes."

I looked quickly for any sort of a landmark. Two houses away, toward the city, there was the number "53" on the front of that dwelling. Across the street from Levere's residence, I saw the number "136." I memorized both of those.

When we reached the end of the next block, I told the driver he could take us back to where we started. We rode in silence. I don't know what Stone was thinking, but I was wondering how I would get his money back.

15

The hackney dropped me off in front of the book shop. I went inside to ask if Pierre Luin visited, only to find him in the process of saying goodbye to Lyle. After catching his eye, I gestured to the stairs. He nodded, and we went up.

"The business will not be as profitable as your other investments, Caz," he said. "But owning this building, in this location, is an opportunity you should not pass up. At some point in the future, Mr. Forteney will wish to retire. When that happens, you can offer the space to someone who will be able to pay a more competitive rent. The book shop can only pay a token amount for the space—no more than ten ducats a month. That equates to only a one percent return."

"What should the rent be for this property?" I asked.

"Including these rooms upstairs, between eighty and a hundred ducats per month," Pierre said. "You do not realize how lucky you are. Mr. Forteney should be charging you at least ten times what you are currently paying."

"The business is profitable?" I asked.

"Yes, but again, not to the level of the other enterprises I have invested my clients' money in. Don't focus on my pessimistic comments," Pierre advised. "Buying the building is something you should do. Keeping the book shop here is your choice. A decent book shop is an asset to a community even though it is not the most lucrative business. With your permission, I can advise Mr. Forteney on how to increase profitability."

"Is he open to advice?" I asked. "I don't want to—"

"He asked," Pierre said. "The reason he started the shop is his love of books. He freely admits he is no businessman. We discussed compensating him on a profit-sharing arrangement. That would make it a better investment for you and mean more money for him."

I said goodbye and thanked Pierre. Not even five minutes later, there was a knock on my door to the outside. Kirk Johanson was standing there, holding a bank draft for fifteen thousand ducats.

"Thank you," he said. "I'm sorry you ended up in the Palace of Justice as a result."

"I was only there briefly," I said graciously. "Sir Oliver let me go."

"He explained that to me when I went to collect the box," Johanson said. "And he would like to see you tomorrow morning."

When Johanson left, I went downstairs to see Lyle. Unfortunately, he left for the day. I climbed back up to my rooms, only to have someone else knock on the door.

"Hello, Freddy," I said with some surprise.

"Come to dinner, Caz," he suggested. "I want to explain this morning."

"Freddy, there's nothing to explain," I said. "You've been very kind about letting me invade your home and mooch breakfast from you the hundreds of times I've done it."

"I don't know if it's hundreds," Freddy said.

"Two or three times a week, for over a year? Hundreds," I replied.

"Well, I don't mind," he said firmly. "I welcome your company. And I felt bad about turning you away. If you'll come to dinner with me, I'll explain why. Now, c'mon. The hackney is waiting."

"Where are we going?" I asked.

"The Equestrian Club."

"Freddy, I'm not dressed appropriately. Can't we just walk over to the Foaming Boar?" I begged.

"Fine," he sighed. "I'll go pay the driver."

I followed Freddy downstairs. He paid the hackney, and we started walking to the inn. Carl found a table for us. It was only after the serving maid brought us mugs of ale that Freddy started to talk.

"The reason I did not let you in was because I had a guest," he said.

"I already figured that out, Freddy," I said with a smile.

"Oh."

"Is it serious?" I asked.

"Serious? No," Freddy grinned. "An actress. I believe you've seen her on stage."

Good for you, Freddy," I said. "And you did the right thing in protecting her modesty. You didn't need to apologize. I understood."

Freddy asked about the scratches he saw on my hands. I shared with him the story of my burglary of Cameron's house, including my almost immediate arrest and subsequent stay in the Palace of Justice. When I mentioned that Sir Oliver wanted to see me the next day, Freddy frowned.

"What do you think he wants?" Freddy asked.

"I think he will caution me that I am dancing too close to the edge of what is legal and what is not," I said. "The problem is that I don't think I will stop any time soon."

After dinner, I contemplated how to retrieve Stone's money. My suspicion was that "Levere" (though I doubted this was his real name) would have the money on hand and not in a bank account. To find out for certain, I would need to get inside his house.

Once inside, what was to stop me from simply taking the money? This did not seem to be a situation where I needed to come up with a ruse or clever stratagem. The problem would be hauling the money away. Six thousand ducats would weigh around six stone. I was fit enough to carry it but would not wish to do so over any considerable distance.

The next morning, I went to the Foaming Boar for a bite to eat. While waiting for my breakfast, I tracked Carl down. He was busy attending to departing guests. When he finished with them, he came over.

"How can I help you, Cap'n?"

"Sar'nt, I need a cosh," I said. "Do you know where I could buy one?"

"Cap'n, I'm not liking the sound of that," he said. "Is this the direction your 'business' is headed? Cracking people on the head?"

"Just this once, Carl," I assured him. "And I hope I don't need it. But if I do…"

"Rather than buy it, would you like to borrow one?" he asked.

"Since I don't think I'll need one in the future, at least not on a regular basis, I'd rather borrow one," I said.

Carl nodded and stood. He crossed to the counter in the common room and reached underneath. When he returned, he laid a leather tube about a foot long onto the table.

Picking it up, it felt as though it was filled with lead pellets. I slapped it against the palm of my hand and quickly regretted doing so. This was exactly what I wanted.

"You won't need it?" I asked.

"I've got a cudgel under there as well," he said. "Haven't needed to use either one in nearly a year. I'll be fine if you bring it back in a day or two."

"I also need a set of lockpicks and some instruction on how to use them," I mentioned.

'Cap'n, you're making me uncomfortable," Carl stated.

I explained how getting Pierre Luin's letters required me to enter the robber's house. He only had a simple latch, but I might encounter more complex locks in the future. I wanted to be prepared when that time came.

"I know a guy," Carl said with some reluctance. "If you're really sure about this, I'll have him stop by."

I took the cosh back to my rooms. My next errand was to visit Sir Oliver. When I returned to the street, a man in nondescript clothing was waiting outside my door.

"May I help you?" I asked.

"Sir Oliver wants to see you," he said. "I'm to take you to him."

"I was just leaving to call upon him," I said. "You're welcome to accompany me if you like."

"I'll do that," he said.

I thought this was a bit heavy-handed of Sir Oliver. Kirk Johanson passed along his request. Did Sir Oliver think I would try to avoid him? Did he see me as a naughty child? Or did he want something from me?

When I arrived at the Palace of Justice, the man accompanying me walked me past the clerk at the end of the entrance hall. We went through the door and up the stairs to Sir Oliver's office. The man knocked.

"Sir Oliver? I've brought FitzDuncan," he said.

That reference irritated me. In response, I entered Sir Oliver's office and sat in one of the chairs facing his desk. I assumed a very relaxed posture with my hands behind my head and my legs crossed as Sir Oliver waved the man away.

"So, I'm just 'FitzDuncan' now? Not 'Mister' FitzDuncan, *Ollie*?" I asked in a snarky tone after the man closed the door.

"*Mister* FitzDuncan," Sir Oliver replied, "please pardon my man's informal tone. I will speak with him about it."

"No need, *Ollie*," I said, deliberately trying to goad him. "He would not have taken the liberty unless that is the way you refer to me when I'm not present. There was no need to send someone after me as though I was a recalcitrant child. Mr. Johanson passed along your request, and I was on my way to see you when I encountered your minion."

"This meeting has gotten off to a horrible start," Sir Oliver said. "I apologize for sending my man. My only defense is that this is a matter of some importance. A situation has come up where I could use your assistance."

"Oh, dear," I said with mock sympathy.

"I already apologized," Sir Oliver snapped.

"Fine," I sighed, sitting up straight. "How may I help you, *Sir* Oliver?"

"We know one of the clerks of courts is taking bribes," Sir Oliver said. "In some recent civil cases brought before the court, he has paid off the juries to ensure a favorable verdict for one side."

"Then arrest him," I said.

"If it were that easy, don't you think I would have done so already?" Sir Oliver snapped. "Sorry. You didn't deserve that. The problem I have is that we have no evidence. Seeking a warrant to search his residence would tip him off and give him the opportunity to hide or destroy the evidence we need to convict him."

"So, you want me to break into the man's house and find evidence of wrongdoing, as I did when I retrieved the letters taken from Madam Saylor?" I asked.

"Yes."

"Sir Oliver, are you aware of my usual terms?"

"If you are referring to your demand to be compensated in the amount of half the value of the recovered item, yes."

"And what is the value of this evidence you want me to find?"

"There is no monetary value we can assign," Sir Oliver said. "This would be a job undertaken for the good of the state."

"In other words, you would like me to risk life and limb to break into this man's house, root around to find evidence of his wrongdoing, and then surrender it to you in exchange for nothing?"

"If you refuse to assist me, I would probably harbor a certain amount of ill will toward you," Sir Oliver said. "I'm only human."

"Ah—there's the stick," I said. "What's the carrot?"

"Your help in resolving this matter would, of course, put you in my good graces," Sir Oliver said with a faint smile.

"But no monetary compensation?" I confirmed.

"No."

"Am I not in your good graces already?" I inquired innocently. "Never mind. The way your man referred to me earlier tells me I am not. Didn't I do you a favor in bringing Madam Saylor's burglar to justice?"

"No," he replied, shaking his head. "You would never have found him without our help. That was a circumstance where both of us benefited equally. Then there was the matter of your illegal entry into Cameron's home."

"Even though I was recovering items that did not belong to the man?" I asked.

"You were not charged with theft," Sir Oliver stated. "You are still guilty of entering the man's home illegally."

"But if I help you with this clerk, won't I be entering his domicile illegally as well?"

"Well, perhaps that might be a circumstance where being in my good graces might be of value to you, don't you think?" Sir Oliver said. "Much as any other illegal entry by you to other places could be viewed harshly or leniently."

"Are you blackmailing me, Sir Oliver?"

"Blackmail is such a nasty word, Mr. FitzDuncan, not to mention that it is a crime," Sir Oliver said blandly. "I'm merely trying to persuade you to be of assistance to the City Watch, as any good citizen of the realm would."

"I would be more inclined to believe that if you approached me in a normal manner," I said, "instead of the heavy-handed way this has progressed so far. How pressing is this issue?"

"We would like to interrupt this clerk before he has the opportunity to influence another jury," Sir Oliver said. "He has no cases pending at the moment. I'll give you the balance of the week to resolve your other matter."

"That's only four days," I remarked. "I have not made up my mind whether I wish to help you."

"I suppose you ought to adjust your thinking quickly, then," Sir Oliver said.

"Just to let you know, I don't respond well to bullying," I said.

He stood, indicating our meeting was over. I left his office, not at all happy about how he was coercing my help. Having Sir Oliver as an enemy and, by extension, the entire City Watch, would make my "profession" more difficult. I did not really have much of a choice. I would help him, but I would make him wait a few days before I caved in.

As I walked back to my rooms, I considered my earlier thinking about how to resolve Mr. Stone's problem. The more I thought about it, the better a bold and direct approach seemed. Before returning to the book shop, I detoured to the livery stable and made arrangements to rent a horse cart the next day.

The following morning, I woke early. After buying a couple of muffins at the bakery, I took the horse cart from the livery. I drove out to the neighborhood where "Levere" lived.

Tying the horse up around the corner, I sauntered down the street, searching for a place where I could keep a discreet watch on Levere's house. I figured there were at least two people living there. When one left, I would make my move.

It was not until midday that I saw the one Mr. Stone identified as Levere leave. I went back and brought the cart to the front of the house. Without knocking, I went in the front door, needing only to fish the latch string out.

"Hello?" I called out.

"Eh?" came a voice from the back room.

"Your front door was open," I said as I moved and positioned myself next to the wall beside the doorway to the back room. "I assume you don't want it left that way.

"Damn right I don't," the man said.

As he stepped through the doorway, I clipped him with the cosh just above his left ear. It made a satisfying thud as I hit him. The man collapsed in a heap.

With him unconscious, I quickly began to search the house. Six thousand ducats would require a chest of decent size or a couple of stout canvas sacks. I found nothing on the first floor.

Aware that the clock was ticking, I climbed to the upper story. My search of those three rooms proved fruitless as well. Just as I returned back down the stairs, the front door opened and the man I knew as Levere stepped in.

Seeing the unconscious body of his associate, and with me on the stairs, he immediately drew his sword. I unsheathed my blade and stepped into the open room. Without a word, Levere attacked.

I fended him off with a ceding parry before sliding my sword along his in a *coulé*. When we were hilt-to-hilt, I punched Levere in the mouth with my left hand. As he staggered back from the blow, I slashed at his throat but he jumped back in time.

Levere recovered and attacked with a *flunge*. I countered with a *croisé*, forcing both our blades down in a *prise de fer*. Releasing quickly, I then attempted a *colpo sottano*. He blocked it using his left arm, but I sliced a deep gash in both his arm and his side, scoring his ribs. As he recoiled from the wound, I rotated and brought the tip of his blade upward, skewering his brain from under his chin.

This was *not* what I wanted to happen. Even worse, the front door was wide open. I hoped no onlookers saw our fight. I would much prefer to have knocked him out, like his accomplice. Unfortunately, instinct honed by years of fighting the Rhetians took over.

After quickly shutting the door, I wracked my brain, trying to figure out where they would have hidden the money, if they indeed had it in the house. I did not want to consider the complications involved in trying to extract it from a bank account, especially with one of the men dead. Thinking about the size and weight of the coins that would make up six thousand ducats, I returned to the kitchen.

I looked for a door to a root cellar. Most homes had one. My idea was that something as heavy as this amount of money would be easier to store on a lower level.

Because I was specifically looking for it this time, I spotted a small trap door. Lifting the cover, I found myself looking down into the root cellar. Even better, I saw two heavy canvas bags of the right size to contain three thousand ducats each.

I flipped the hatch covering the entrance to the cellar and stepped to where the ladder was. That saved my life. The man I knocked out with the cosh had recovered and took a swipe at me.

He missed me entirely. Dancing around the open cellar, I pulled my own blade. Whether because he was still dazed from the blow I delivered to his head or was simply not skilled with a blade, I dispatched him easily. My mistake in killing his partner forced me to do the same here. I had no desire to kill either man, but did not wish to leave a witness alive.

After cleaning my blade on his shirt and sheathing it, I climbed down into the cellar and heaved the two canvas sacks up. I carried them outside to the cart, one at a time. After I loaded the second, I made sure the front door of the house was shut, then drove off.

16

I took the two sacks to Farmer & Mercantile. After counting the contents, they found exactly six thousand ducats. This didn't surprise me. Both were stenciled with "Bannister Brothers"—the name of another prominent bank, and both were cinched closed with the sort of thongs banks used.

I deposited three thousand in my account and asked the bank to write a draft for three thousand. With that in hand, I returned the cart to the livery. The man at the livery looked at me strangely.

"What?" I asked.

"Uh," he let out, then pointed at my breeches.

There was a large bloodstain on my right thigh. Fortunately, it was not my blood. Embarrassingly, if the man at the livery noticed it, I was sure the folks at Farmer & Mercantile did as well. I returned home, changed clothes, and then went in search of Mr. Stone.

His manservant gave me directions to Stone's office. He looked surprised to see me so soon. I handed over the bank draft.

"That was quick," he commented.

"It wasn't a complicated problem," I replied.

My blithe response did not match my true feelings. I had only wanted to retrieve the money. Leaving two dead bodies in my wake was not what I intended. Even though they were both criminals, their transgressions hardly merited their deaths.

I slept poorly that night. My troubled conscience kept me awake. The next morning, I intended to wheedle breakfast out of Freddy. Perhaps by confessing what I did, I would feel better.

When I exited the building, the same man who took me to the Palace of Justice the day before was waiting for me again. He didn't say anything, merely jerking his head over his shoulder in the direction of the Palace of Justice. I followed him, trapped in my gloomy and remorseful mood.

As before, we marched past the clerk at the end of the entrance hall. He led me up the stairs. After knocking and hearing Sir Oliver's response, he opened the door and stood aside.

"Mr. FitzDuncan," Sir Oliver said expansively. "You certainly did not waste a moment of time in resolving things for your client. I appreciate your eagerness to begin working on my request. You might consider exercising more discretion in the future. Your approach this time was as subtle as a battering ram."

"Excuse me?" I asked, pretending an innocence I did not feel at all.

"Come, come, now," he said. "False modesty does not suit you. With regard to your subtlety, you left two bodies behind, showed up at Farmer & Mercantile with their blood soaking your breeches, then delivered his share of the recovered loot to Mr. Barclay Stone."

"Are you having me followed, Sir Oliver?" I asked.

"Oh, that would be telling," he teased. "But since you completed your task for Mr. Stone so quickly, there is no time like the present to tackle my request."

"Sir Oliver, I haven't even agreed to help you yet," I protested, even though I knew that if Sir Oliver knew of the two deaths, I would have no choice.

"You must be joking," he said. "You left my office and killed two people the very next day. I'm prepared to overlook breaking and entering. Murder? I'm not sure I can let that pass."

"It was self-defense, I assure you," I said more calmly than I felt, perhaps even hoping I might reassure myself of that.

"There were no witnesses to the actual confrontation, but I feel confident we can find someone who will place you at the scene," Sir Oliver said. "Finding others who can attest to your bloodstained appearance will be no problem, and some of them have already come forward. There are two dead bodies, and you entered the house while at least one of them was alive. I'll be happy to have my men toss you in a cell while we investigate the deaths. I'm sure a jury will find it easy to understand that you killed those two men for their money. Is that what you want?"

"No, Sir Oliver," I said. "If it makes any difference to you, I was planning to help you regardless, after making you wait a few days because I did not appreciate your attempt to intimidate me. And, lest you think I am some cold-blooded assassin, I did not set out yesterday with any thought of killing those two men. At most, I planned on giving one of them a headache."

"My man saw the bruise that started to form on the one's head," Sir Oliver commented. "What went wrong?"

"It took me too long to find where they hid the money," I said. "I entered the house after the one man—who used the name Levere with Mr. Stone—departed. Then I knocked the other out. I wanted to find the money and leave before Levere returned."

"Instead, he came back and drew on you," Sir Oliver guessed. "Why did you kill him? After seven years in the Rangers, I would imagine you are quite skilled with a blade—skilled enough to disable him without ending his life."

"You're right," I admitted. "Sadly, he was just good enough that my reflexes took over. I had no desire to kill him. When his partner regained consciousness, I did not feel it would be prudent to leave a witness alive."

"So, here we are," Sir Oliver said. "I can have my man show you where the clerk lives. You won't need to worry about being disturbed—court is in session. It will be hours before the clerk returns."

"Doing this will restore me to your good graces?" I asked.

"Doing this will keep you out of prison for murder," Sir Oliver said. "You will still be greatly indebted to me."

"I understand," I sighed, upset with myself that I created the uncomfortable situation I was now in. "In the future, Sir Oliver, rest assured I will be happy to provide my assistance if you merely ask. There is no need to try to browbeat me. Recent unfortunate event aside, I consider myself a good person and a loyal citizen."

"I have little doubt of that, Mr. FitzDuncan," Sir Oliver said, "but I would be a fool not to take advantage of your mistakes. My man will take you to the clerk's residence."

"And what is it you expect me to find?" I asked.

"A ledger?" Sir Oliver posited. "Some written record of the cases he has influenced."

The man who met me outside the book shop was waiting in the corridor. I followed him out of the building and into a neighborhood not too different from the one where Levere lived. We stopped at an apartment building.

"Third floor, right side," was all the man said.

I entered the building and climbed the two flights of stairs. At the landing, I paused and looked out the window. Sir Oliver's man was still across the street. I caught his eye and pointed at the room on his right. He nodded.

There was no lock on the door. I opened it and entered. There was not much to it—only two small rooms. I decided to start with his bedroom.

My mood was foul. I was none too gentle in how I conducted my search. First, I tore the covers off his bed and flipped the mattress to see if he had hidden anything there. I searched underneath for a loose floorboard.

Then I began pulling the drawers out of a dresser along the wall. I dumped the contents on the floor and kicked them to see if there were any papers. When I pulled out the bottom drawer and emptied it, I found what I was looking for. Underneath the lowest drawer, lying on the bottom shelf of the dresser, was a packet of papers.

I looked through them quickly to make sure that I had the right material. There were entries that I guessed corresponded to different cases, and then under them, there were different names listed, with numbers next to them. I reckoned those were the amounts of the bribes since they were multiples of five. The smallest amount was twenty, while the largest was a hundred.

Just to be sure, I went through the front room as well. I left behind a wake of disorder there, too. There was nothing more to find, so I left with the packet under my arm. Leaving the building, I gave the papers to Sir Oliver's man and headed back to my rooms in a thoroughly rotten frame of mind.

Looking back on it later, I figured out that what I wanted was comfort—reassurance that I was not a bad person. I'd been helping my "clients," and in this most recent case, helped Mr. Stone, but in the other situations, I did not injure anyone. The only harm I caused was to recover items that did not rightfully belong to my "victims."

My need for comfort and reassurance—even though I was not able to articulate it to myself so neatly at the time—is what pushed me to take the step I decided to take. I resolved that I would visit my mother.

My memories of her were extremely hazy and only fragments. Antonia—that was her name—left Easton Manor when my father's marriage to Veronica was arranged. I was only three.

My grandfather settled her in the town of Hiram, near the port of Aurora. He told me that he provided her with a small sum to get started. I understood she established herself as a seamstress.

On my way back to my rooms I stopped by the office of the Royal Post to see how close they could get me to Hiram. I was in luck. The route the post followed to reach Aurora went through Hiram.

The coach would leave the city early the next morning. Six days later, I would arrive in Hiram. I went to my rooms and filled my valise with clothes. When I finished, I spoke with Lyle Forteney, informing him that I would be out of the city for a couple of weeks in the event anyone came looking for me.

The journey to Hiram was not pleasant. Traveling anywhere by post coach is uncomfortable. Still, it was cheap and much quicker than walking.

The driver delivered me to the lone inn in the town. It was midafternoon, so I decided not to seek my mother out so late in the day. I obtained a room and spent the rest of the day reading a book I borrowed for the trip—something I found impossible to do in the coach during the trip. Trying to focus on the page would make me nauseous.

After breakfast the next morning, I asked the innkeeper where I might find Antonia, the seamstress. I realized I did not know my mother's last name. Luckily, he knew who she was and exactly where she lived. The only problem was that his directions were a bit confusing.

I left the inn and tried to follow the innkeeper's instructions, but I was not at all sure I was in the right place when I finished. There was no sign above any door indicating the presence of a seamstress. Having no other choice, I went to the door of the nearest small house and knocked.

"Yes?" the woman who came to the door asked.

"Excuse me," I said. "I'm looking for Antonia? The seamstress?"

"And who might you be?" the woman said suspiciously.

"A relative," I responded.

"Don't see much family resemblance," the woman said.

"That might be," I stated, "but we are related."

"Huh," she grunted skeptically. "She lives over there," she said as she pointed across the lane and two doors down.

"Thank you, ma'am," I said.

After crossing to the door that the woman indicated, I stopped for a moment. I realized I had no idea how my mother would react to seeing me, more than two decades later. For that matter, I did not know how seeing her would make me feel. I nearly turned around but instead stepped forward and knocked.

"Just a moment!" I heard someone call from within.

A few seconds later, I heard footsteps. The door opened, revealing a slender woman of moderate height. Her nearly black hair contained a few strands of gray. She was close to fifty years old, but her features were still attractive. It was easy to imagine that she was a beauty in her youth, and I understood how my father would not have been able to resist temptation.

"Are you Antonia?" I asked.

"Yes. And you are?"

"Casimir."

With that, her eyes rolled up in her head. She fainted right in front of me. It happened so fast that I was not able to catch her as she slumped to the floor. Fortunately, she did not hit her head when she fell.

I stepped inside. Not knowing exactly what to do, having never seen a woman faint before, I picked her up. I looked for somewhere to place her. There was nothing in the front room.

Her bedroom was off to the side. I carried her in there and placed her on her bed. Kneeling beside her, I held her hand and rubbed it until, a few minutes later, her eyes fluttered open. She sat up.

"Majors and Minors!" she gasped as her eyes found mine. "I thought I would never see you again. What in creation drove you to come find me? And why now?"

"I apologize for not coming sooner, Mother," I said.

"Say that again," she requested.

"Which part?"

"The last word you said."

"Yes, Mother," I said with a smile.

Tears started to roll down her cheeks. She began to sob. Like all men, I am helpless when confronted with a crying woman. I could think of nothing else to do except lean forward and embrace her.

It took her a few minutes to regain her composure. Eventually, she leaned back. Reaching into a pocket of her dress, she withdrew a handkerchief. She dried her eyes and blew her nose with a noisy honk.

"Oh, what you must think of me," she moaned. "Help me up. We'll go to the front room. I'll fix some tea, and we'll talk, right?"

"That sounds just fine," I said.

I stood up and offered her my hand. She took it and got on her feet. When she did, she turned to me, holding me by my upper arms and looking at me intently.

"Come along," she said, stepping past me. "Sit down. I'll make us some tea. There's nothing like a cup of tea to settle jangled nerves."

She disappeared into the back room, which I assumed was the kitchen. I sat on a chair that looked comfortable. She returned and looked at me closely once again.

"You look like your father did at the same age," she said. "You must get tired of hearing that."

"You're the first person to mention it," I said. "I haven't seen my father in nearly a decade—not since grandfather's funeral."

"What?"

I then explained as best I could what happened after she was sent away, including my own exile after Veronica gave birth to Edwin. At this point, the kettle began to whistle. She jumped up, wiping her eyes as she did, and bustled into the kitchen.

She spent more time in the kitchen than preparing two cups of tea would require. When she reappeared, her eyes were redder than before. I then resumed my story, telling her of being sent away to school and only being allowed to return to Easton for my grandfather's funeral.

"That was the last time I saw my father," I said, "and then only from a distance."

"That's cruel," she said. "I do not remember either your father or his father ever displaying any sign of cruelty. It must have been your stepmother's doing."

"That would be my guess as well," I said.

I resumed telling her my story—of my time at school and in the Rangers. When I reached my journey to the city of Aquileia after leaving the Rangers, I stopped. The look on her face was one of anguish.

"I'm so sorry, Casimir," she said. "So very, very sorry. I wanted to take you with me, but your grandfather forbade it. He felt you would have a better life growing up at the manor than what I could provide. It sounds as though it did not turn out the way he hoped, thanks to that woman."

"I wouldn't know," I admitted. "With my father absent most of the time and keeping his distance from me when he was home, grandfather raised me until he sent me away. Actually, grandfather and the armsmen. Enough about me. How has your life been?"

"Your grandfather made sure I would be comfortable," she said. "I get a hundred ducats a year from an account with Farmer & Mercantile Bank. In addition, I have my business as a seamstress. The people here in Hiram accepted me when I arrived, and I have friends."

"You never married?" I asked.

"After being sent away and leaving you behind, I was not of a mind to take up with anyone," she said. "By the time I was ready to consider it, a few years later, there was no longer anyone of the right age who was interested. I had my business and made friends, so I have not been lonely."

The next day, when I stopped by again, she said, "It is kind of you to have sought me out. But it is also painful for me. Even though I gave birth to you, I am not your mother any more than Veronica is. What's done is done. We cannot rewrite the past."

"You don't want to see me again?" I asked.

"It is enough for me to know you are doing well," she said with a pained smile.

I spent the rest of the day with her. When the post coach came through Hiram the next morning, I waved it down. Six days later, I returned to my rooms above the book shop.

- 143 -

17

Spending another six days in the post coach had me almost convinced that I wanted to buy a horse so I never needed to endure such torture. After I returned to my rooms above the book shop, I unpacked my valise. I was about to head to the shop to ask Lyle to have the lads prepare a bath for me when there was a knock at the door. Answering, I saw the same watchman who summoned me to see Sir Oliver twice before.

"Your presence is requested," the man said.

"Requested or commanded?" I asked.

He shrugged.

"Immediately?"

"Sir Oliver has been wondering where you have been. He did not appreciate that you left the city without explanation," he said.

I nearly barked at the man, intending to complain that, as a free man, I could go anywhere I pleased, but I realized he was just a messenger. Instead, I choked back my irritation. I gave him a shrug like the one he'd given me.

"Fine. Let's go."

"Mr. FitzDuncan, so nice to see you," Sir Oliver said when I entered his office.

"I wish I could say the same," I replied. "You do understand I just spent the last six days in a post coach and only arrived back in the city just over an hour ago?"

"I knew you would be eager to learn of how you helped bring a criminal to justice," Sit Oliver said. "So, I brought you here immediately."

"While I am mildly curious, I would have been happy to wait," I said.

"I, on the other hand, have been dying to tell you. *Dying to*," he stressed.

"You made your point, *Ollie*," I replied.

"Good. I was hoping your absence of two weeks did not cause you to forget. Our mutual friend, the clerk, never filed a complaint of burglary," Sir Oliver said. "Imagine that!"

I rolled my eyes in response.

"Immediately after you left the city, my people began visiting the jurors listed in the papers you found. At the same time, he left the city and headed to Newcastle. We followed him for three days. My people in the city had that long to gather sworn statements from the jurors on his list. Then, we dragged the clerk back to the city and threw him in a cell. He is currently awaiting trial."

"That's nice," I said in a bored tone.

"You'll never imagine what his attorney asked first," Sir Oliver said.

"Please enlighten me," I replied in the same bored manner.

"He wanted to know what the basis for our charges was. When we told him that we had sworn testimony from jurors whom the clerk bribed, the lawyer wanted to know how we knew to contact those people. I swear, the man was about to burst a blood vessel when I told him that someone anonymously left a document for us that listed trials, jurors, and the amounts of the bribes he paid. He accused me of conducting an illegal search of the man's premises. I was able to state truthfully that such was not the case."

"Is this news the only reason you summoned me?" I asked.

"Well, that, and to find out where you went," Sit Oliver asked.

"Oh," I said with mock surprise that he would be interested. "That's easy. I went to *none of your business*, Sir Oliver. I'm sure you've heard of the place. It's just down the road from *tend your own garden*, and across the river from *it doesn't concern you*."

"Excuse me, *Mister* FitzDuncan, but when a citizen goes on a murderous rampage, I think I'm entitled to keep track of his whereabouts," Sit Oliver snapped.

"I told you before that I had no intention of killing anyone that day. If I started my search in the root cellar instead of the second floor, I would have been long gone before Levere returned. I would have preferred that greatly to what happened."

"His name was Callahan. The other man was Cheatham," Sir Oliver said. "In case you want to know who you murdered."

"Murder implies malice aforethought," I objected. "These deaths were unfortunate accidents of timing."

"But you did kill two men who, while career criminals, did not deserve death as their punishment," he said. "In the future, until I say otherwise, please check with me before leaving the city."

"Am I not a free man?" I asked.

"Consider yourself a prisoner on parole," Sir Oliver replied.

"And how long will it take until you say otherwise?" I asked.

"If you manage to make it through the next year without another killing spree, I will agree that what happened was, as you phrased it, 'an unfortunate accident of timing.' On the other hand, if you create any more corpses, your parole will be revoked. And, just to make myself clear, when and if I need you for further errands of the sort you just completed for me, you will be at my beck and call."

"So, I may not leave the city without your permission," I stated. "I am, in effect, a prisoner."

"You could be a prisoner in one of our many cells a few floors down," Sir Oliver said. "I can arrange that if you wish."

"No, thank you," I said through gritted teeth. "I will play by your rules. If I have a client who needs my assistance outside of the city, I will come to you before leaving the city."

"As long as you understand that I may not grant you permission to leave," Sir Oliver said. "Chances are that I will have no problem approving your travel, but one never knows."

"Sir Oliver, was it the timing of my departure that troubled you?" I asked. "Did you think I was running away?"

"Yes."

"Then I will share with you where I went in the hope that it puts your mind at ease," I said. "What happened with Levere, or Callahan—whatever his name was—troubled me enough that I decided to travel to visit my mother. The last time I saw her was when I was three years old."

"Majors and Minors! I did not know," Sir Oliver stated in surprise when he saw I was serious. "I knew from your surname that… But I had no idea you grew up without a mother."

"She was sent away when my father married," I said. "Just as I was banished when my stepmother gave birth to her first."

I then proceeded to share with Sir Oliver the abbreviated story of my upbringing. From his reaction, he knew none of it before. All he understood prior to this was that I was the illegitimate son of the Earl of the Eastern March.

"Mr. FitzDuncan—" he began when I finished.

"My friends call me Caz," I interrupted. "Please feel free to do the same."

"Caz," he said carefully, as though trying on a new jacket, "I have known other noble bastards before. They grew up to be both spoiled and bitter. It's a volatile combination. I assumed you were cut from the same cloth. It seems that might not be the case. Here's what I ask. Treat me and this office with respect, and I will endeavor to extend the same courtesy to you. That does not, however, mean that your parole is over. Do you understand?"

"Under the circumstances, that seems fair," I agreed.

He stood and offered me his hand for the first time since I barged into his office initially. I took it, and we shook. That was also my cue to depart.

The next morning, I headed over to Freddy's to mooch breakfast from him. Roger let me in. When I went back to where Freddy was sprawled on the sofa, he squinted at me.

"It's been more than two weeks since you last sponged breakfast, Caz," he grumbled. "Where have you been?"

I shared all the details of what I'd done with Freddy, pausing only when Roger served our breakfast. It was clear Freddy was distressed when I told him about killing the two men. He was even more affected when I shared the story of visiting my mother.

"If you want a family, Caz, we will take you in. We already consider you one of ours," he said. "That has been the case since your first visit to Manton. All you ever need to do is reach out."

I'm not ashamed to say that I started crying. Part of the reason was the truth of it. The summer I spent with Freddy's family, they treated me as one of them, not as a guest. They gave me chores to do, no more or less pleasant than the ones assigned to Freddy. I didn't mind being expected to work. It made me feel a sense of belonging. Plus, Freddy and I found ways to get into mischief nearly every day.

Later, when I had the chance to reflect, I considered that it had been much the same with Linc Ellsworth's family when I spent the summer with them in Bergin, and with the Hawkinses the time I spent the winter holidays. Both of their families made me feel like any other member. I realized the Gods blessed me with the best of friends. I might not have large numbers of them, but I could not ask for better people to have on my side.

"I think you need a good drunk, Caz," Freddy said when I regained my composure. "I'll arrange everything. Just show up here around six o'clock this evening, dressed well."

"Freddy—" I tried to protest.

"No! Listen to Doctor Austermain," he said imperiously. "I have diagnosed what is ailing you, and alcohol in immoderate quantity is my prescription. You need to get google-eyed—there's just nothing else for it."

They tell me I had a very good time. I don't remember much, and what I do recall is brief flashes, like Ratty trying to sing as we stumbled back to Freddy's. In the morning, I woke on the floor of Freddy's sitting room as Freddy came downstairs in his dressing gown, whistling.

Linc Ellsworth was on the sofa. Ratty Hawkins was stretched out on the floor not far away. The sound of Freddy's whistling was entirely too cheerful for the three of us. We made a brief attempt to shout at him to be quiet, but the yelling hurt our heads even more.

"How can you be so damned happy?" Ratty moaned.

"Oh, I feel just as collywobbled as you three," Freddy admitted, "but I'm pretending I don't. I'm trying to fool my body into believing that all is well."

"Freddy, you were supposed to remind me," I groaned.

"Remind you of what, Caz?"

"Not to play drinking games with Linc."

"Yes, that's usually sound advice," Freddy admitted, "but in your case, Doctor Austermain felt it was the proper treatment for the case of the megrims you were mired in. I'll bet you've already forgotten all your troubles."

"My head is pounding so hard I can't even think," I said.

"See?" Freddy stated triumphantly.

"Would the two of you be quiet?" Ratty whined. "I'm trying to fall back asleep. Maybe this is only a bad dream, and I'll wake up feeling fine."

"That's not a bad idea, Ratty," Linc mumbled.

"Breakfast is served, milord," Roger said then.

"Spit-spot, men," Freddy ordered. "Roger has prepared a number of delicacies specifically chosen to soothe your troubled guts. To the table!"

The idea of eating anything caused my stomach to twitch. Fortunately, I knew if I could keep it down, it would speed my recovery. With a groan, I hoisted myself off the floor and stumbled after Freddy. Linc and Ratty stayed where they were.

Reaching the table, I flopped into a chair. True to what Freddy described, there was fruit, oatmeal, lean bacon, and eggs. There were also carafes of water. I helped myself to some of the oatmeal and added pieces of fruit. Taking small bites slowly, I allowed my guts time to adapt to the invasion, drinking plenty of water along the way.

By the time I finished, I felt prepared to stumble my way back to my rooms without assistance. Ratty and Linc were both back asleep. I said goodbye to Freddy.

"I'll say 'thank you,' but you'll need to tell me later how much fun I had since I can't remember," I joked.

"We had a marvelous time, Caz," Freddy assured me. "Any evening when Ratty favors us with song is a good one."

"I only vaguely remember Ratty singing," I admitted.

"That's a good thing," Freddy said with a grin. "I wish I could forget."

With that I walked away chuckling despite my precarious physical condition. When I returned to the book shop, I demanded my weekly bath. Lyle was prepared to begin bantering with me until he observed how hungover I was.

I fell asleep in the tub. When I woke in the now-cold water, the combination of the breakfast I ate along with sweating out the poison when the bath was hot had me feeling almost human again. I won't say I was in a chipper mood, but my outlook was much improved.

Not long after this, the winter holidays arrived. Linc Ellsworth invited me to his annual party. The year before, I went with Celeste Nash, now Celeste Mellon. I was hesitant about going, but Freddy, Ratty, and Linc all prevailed upon me to attend.

When I arrived, the party was in full swing. Freddy caught my eye and waved me over. He was with a group of people and attempted to introduce me.

"Caz, I'd like you to meet George Westhaver and his wife, Louella," Freddy said. Before Freddy finished his sentence, Westhaver and his wife turned their backs to me and began walking away. Freddy frowned.

"That's rather ill-mannered," Freddy growled quietly.

"It's nothing new, Freddy," I said.

He tried again later with the Duke of Namie and his wife, Eudora. They did not turn their backs on me, but a three-day dead fish had more life in it than the handshake I received from the duke. His wife did not offer her hand to me at all.

"What's wrong with these people?" Freddy said exasperatedly.

"They will never associate with anyone whose surname begins with Fitz," Linc said, coming up from behind us. "I'm sorry, Caz. If I knew what Freddy was doing, I would have warned him off."

"Why did you invite such horrid people?" Freddy asked.

"This is my parents' party," Linc explained. "I'm allowed to include my friends, but most of the guest list comes from them."

"There is no possible way that your parents are close to those people," Freddy said.

"They're not, thank all the heavenly beings," Linc said, "but they do try to be inclusive. It's the holidays—blessings of the Gods to men of good will and all that. See that group over there?"

"What about them?" Freddy asked.

"Don't bother trying to introduce Caz to any of them," Linc said. "They're all a bunch of self-important snots. Except for the two Braintrees in that crowd, none of them hold territories worth a damn. You could replace any one of them with a scarecrow, and the only effect would be that their people might be better off."

"Then why so high and mighty?" Freddy asked.

"Because their families have controlled their worthless holdings for hundreds of years," Linc said. "None of them have any influence with the king, which makes them bitter."

"Freddy, this is nothing new," I said. "We went to school with several of them, and they acted the same way then."

"You would think they would grow out of such behavior," Freddy remarked.

"Hardly," Linc said with a laugh. "The juice from their vines ages into vinegar, not wine."

"That's quite clever, Linc," I said. "Do you mind if I steal it and use it when you're not around?"

"Feel free," he chuckled. "I'll try to come up with some more. That was one of my better ones, though."

I departed not long after. What happened cast a pall over my mood, and I was not very good company. I ended up walking home as snow began to fall.

18

That winter was one where I had no new "clients." I was able to enjoy a life of leisure—playing cards with Freddy and the others, visiting the salle to stay fit, and reading voraciously. That ended near the equinox when a man approached me on the recommendation of Barclay Stone.

Jude Mathis' problem was not much different from the one Kirk Johanson brought to me. There was some jewelry willed to him by his late father. When the father died, he left most of his estate to Jude, despite Jude being the younger brother. His older brother, Vincent, refused to abide by the terms of the will.

There were three items of great value. One was the house in which Vincent was living and would not leave. He would not allow Jude inside. Jude was pursuing legal remedies for that. Another was the bank account, which Vincent already drained. Again, Jude was going through the courts to resolve that issue. The third problem was the family jewels.

"Is there any staff in the house who could give you access?" I asked. "That would solve your problems quickly."

"There is a housekeeper," Mathis said, "but she is an older woman. Vincent is a large man. He uses his size to intimidate people. She is scared he will hurt her."

"You have used the courts for the house and the bank accounts," I said. "Why not the jewels?"

"My fear is that Vincent will sell them soon," Jude explained. "When he does, the only way I will have to recover them will be to buy them back from the person to whom he sells them. That will be outrageously expensive, and there is no guarantee I will be successful in regaining all of them."

"You're aware of my terms?" I asked.

"Yes. The entire collection is worth roughly ten thousand ducats," he said. "Vincent is such a boneheaded dunce that he would take them to a pawnbroker instead of a reputable jeweler and get only half that. Then, trying to buy them back would cost more."

"How so?" I asked.

"Have you ever done business with a pawnbroker?" Mathis asked.

"No."

"I swear they have a sixth sense about things," Mathis stated. "If they know that there is a specific item that you need to obtain, the price will be astronomical. The five thousand I will pay you will be far less than what it will cost me to recover them from pawnbrokers."

"For now, you believe the jewels are still in the house?" I asked.

"As far as I know," Mathis said, "Vincent has not left the premises since he withdrew my father's money from the bank."

"But you think he will soon?"

"Yes. The court served him a writ today regarding the bank account," Mathis said. "That will make him nervous about the jewelry. I think he will try to sell it soon."

"You mentioned that Vincent is a 'boneheaded dunce'—is that the phrase?"

"Yes. He has a number of negative qualities," Mathis said. "He's not bright at all, he's suspicious, he's sneaky, and he would rather lie than tell the truth. It helps if you think of him as having the mental age of a naughty ten-year-old boy."

"Did your father make *any* provision in the will for him?" I asked.

"Not in terms of specific assets," Mathis said, "but my father requested in the will that I take care of Vincent, which I intend to do. I doubt my brother would be able to live on his own."

"Where do you think the jewelry is?" I asked.

"There was a vanity in my parents' bedroom that was my mother's," Mathis said. "After she died, my father never touched it. Her jewelry box was in the top drawer. Vincent has probably taken it and moved it into his bedroom."

"And the housekeeper can't let me in?" I asked.

"He has not allowed her to answer the door. I've tried sending neighbors and friends," he said.

"So, in order to retrieve the jewelry box, I will need to break into the house and then get to his bedroom. Is that right?"

"Yes."

"Let's go see where your house is," I said.

It was pouring down rain when we left my rooms. I put on an oilskin. Mathis had only a regular cloak.

"Perhaps we should hire a hackney," I suggested.

"I think so," he admitted. "It was not raining when I arrived."

The ride in the hackney took only a couple of minutes. The Mathis house was in the same part of town as Freddy's. There was a short fence at the side of the lane and a small garden in front. On either side was a narrow grassy area separating the house from its neighbors.

I directed the driver to circle around to the service alley behind the house. Most houses extended to the alley. Mathis's was no exception. I examined the back of the house carefully, looking to see where it would be easiest to get in. I still did not have a set of lockpicks. Though I meant to get one, the man Carl knew had not yet provided them. I reminded myself to ask Sir Oliver, thinking that would probably thrill him.

The back door had a lock and looked sturdy. There were two windows on both the first and second floors. The first floor windows were too high to reach from the ground. A downspout came down on each corner. Looking at it, I thought I could reach the window if I stretched.

"Is your brother's room in the back or front of the house?" I asked.

"The one on the right," Mathis said.

I asked the driver to take us back to the book shop. While we were on the way, I was considering how I would get into the house. By the time we arrived, I had decided I could do this.

"Mr. Mathis, I'll help you out," I said.

"Please hurry," he urged.

It rained that evening. As I had no desire to try to shinny up the downspout when it was wet, I stayed in. In the morning, after stopping at a bakery for an apple fritter, which I ate while I walked, I went to the Palace of Justice.

A new man was at the desk at the end of the entrance corridor. I simply walked past him as though I belonged there. He didn't stop me. I climbed the stairs and knocked on Sir Oliver's door before walking in.

Sir Oliver gave me an annoyed look. Spurred by that, I sprawled in the chair facing his desk the way Freddy would have. He waited for me to speak. I said nothing.

"What?" he demanded finally.

"Hasn't your man told you that Mr. Jude Mathis visited me yesterday?" I asked.

"Oh. That," Sir Oliver said.

His tone of voice conveyed that he knew about Mathis's visit and did not care. I wondered whether he was having one of his men watch me. Deciding that his doing so would be a use of City Watch resources better employed elsewhere, I reckoned he paid one of Lyle's two employees. While that irritated me, I kept my cool. There might be a way I could make that work in my favor sometime in the future.

"Mr. Mathis has engaged my service to retrieve some jewelry that was left to him in his father's will," I explained.

I provided Sir Oliver with the details of the situation. He nodded when I told him that the matter of the house and the father's bank account were being handled by the courts. I shared with him Mathis's fear that his brother would pawn the jewels.

"What do you intend to do about it?" Sir Oliver asked.

"Shinny up the downspout, open a window and go through it, incapacitate Vincent Mathis, take the jewelry back, and walk out the door," I said.

"When you say, 'incapacitate,' you mean to restrain him in some way, correct? A temporary incapacitation and not a permanent one, Caz?"

"That is my great preference, Ollie," I said.

"Well, good luck," Sir Oliver said.

"That's all?" I asked.

"I certainly cannot condone breaking and entering," Sir Oliver said. "So, if you were hoping for my approval, you'll leave disappointed."

"Will you prevent me from helping my client?" I asked.

"No. I will pretend this was merely a social call," he said.

"A courtesy," I suggested. "Considering I am on parole."

"Indeed. Don't get me wrong, Caz," he said. "I do appreciate your prudence in letting me know your plans in advance. It's possible I may position someone where he could hear a ruckus—such as furniture breaking, that kind of thing. Otherwise, he'll stay in the shadows. After all, I can't have you going on another murderous rampage. In the future, you will not need to share details about your illicit activities. Just let me know if you plan to leave the city."

"Or if I plan on killing someone," I quipped.

"That, too."

After leaving the Palace of Justice, I stopped by the Foaming Boar. I borrowed Carl's cosh again. He handed it over with a strange expression.

"Keep it," he said. "You have more need of it than I do."

"At least let me pay you for it," I said.

"Fine," he said, rolling his eyes. "Twelve florins."

"That's all?"

"I made it myself, Cap'n," he admitted. "I have no idea what it cost. Probably nowhere near that much."

"Fine," I said with a laugh.

I counted out the coins and handed them over. Slipping the sap into my pocket, I returned to the book shop. I stopped in, ostensibly to pick out a used book to read but really to look at the two young men Lyle employed. One of them, if not both of them, was telling Sir Oliver of my comings and goings. From my brief examination, I could not tell which one it was so I decided both of them were in on it.

I waited until I heard the clock in the square strike one that night. Wearing the darkest clothing I owned, I set out for the Mathis house. I left my sword at home. Climbing up a downspout and wiggling through a window, it would just get in the way. I'd brought some leather thongs that I would use to tie Vincent up and a handkerchief to stuff in his mouth as a gag to keep him from yelling.

There was a last-quarter moon, low in the sky. It would give me enough light to see but not so much that it would give me away unless someone was looking for me. It took me roughly ten minutes to reach the service alley behind the Mathis house. I spent another five minutes making sure nothing and no one was stirring nearby.

The downspout was made of cast iron. I tested to see how securely it was attached to the house. It did not wiggle at all. I took that as a good sign.

Pulling myself up with my hands and squeezing with my knees, I reached the second floor. Earlier, I decided I would try the window in Vincent's room first. The distance between the downspout and the window was farther than I had estimated. Switching from one to the other would be much riskier than I thought.

After a brief debate with myself, whether to try to reach across with my hands, or stretch my leg over, I climbed high enough to use my legs. Still clinging to the downspout, I reached with my left leg. I could feel my toe on the sill, and was not fully extended. That was good.

I took some deep breaths to calm myself. When I was ready, I made my move. It was not quite a leap, but for a moment the only contact I had with the house was with my toes on the windowsill.

The fingers of my left hand grasped the upper part of the window frame, followed by my right. My grip was solid, and I breathed a soundless sigh of relief. My right foot followed.

I stood still, listening to see if my quiet movement disturbed Vincent inside. The sound of his regular slow breathing reassured me that he was still sound asleep. I shifted my grip to the side of the window frame with my right hand. With my left hand, I sought a purchase, trying to open the sash on the left.

I had no luck. Though there was no mullion in the middle of the two sashes, they were latched shut. I pulled my knife from my boot and slid it between the sashes. Working it upward slowly, I reached the latch and lifted it.

After putting my knife away, I tried the left-hand side again. It opened easily and quietly. My ears were straining the entire time, listening to the sound of Vincent sleeping.

I stepped to the left and opened the right side of the window. After looking inside to make sure there was no furniture waiting to trip me up, I slid in. I debated whether I should try to tie Vincent up while he was asleep, or tap him with the cosh and make sure he slept for a long time.

Using the cosh seemed the safer choice. I crossed to the bed. Vincent was sleeping on his left side, facing away from the window. I gave him a sharp rap above the ear. He grunted softly, but his breathing soon returned to its earlier rhythm.

Rolling him onto his stomach, I fastened his hands behind his back with the leather thongs. I used others on his feet. There did not seem to be a reason to gag him, so I did not.

After I found a candle, I struck a spark and lit it. That made my job easier. The jewelry box was not in sight.

I dropped to my knees at the foot of the bed. Jude's description of his brother as behaving like a boy of ten guided my thinking. A naughty boy of that age would think hiding things under a loose floorboard below the bed would be the height of cleverness. Feeling around, I quickly found the floorboard.

I reached inside and immediately felt a box. After pulling it out, I opened it and looked inside. From the description Jude gave me, it seemed as though nothing was missing.

While there were probably other items stashed away in Vincent's hidey-hole, what would be attractive to someone with the mental and emotional age of ten was not something I wanted to stick my hand into. Tucking the box into my jacket, I checked on Vincent. Hearing his deep, regular breath, I decided to untie the thongs around his wrists and ankles.

That done, I tiptoed out of the room. Remembering the lesson Sir Oliver's man taught me when I retrieved Pierre Luin's letters, I stayed to the outside of the corridor and stepped on the stair treads close to the wall. I managed to avoid making much noise and slipped out the front door without anyone raising the alarm.

I made my way back to my rooms and went to sleep. The next morning, with the box under my jacket and an oilskin on top to protect me from the rain that was falling, I set off the find Jude Mathis. I was early enough that I hoped he might feed me breakfast.

His man let me in, and Mathis did invite me in for a bite to eat. He was pleased to see that all the jewelry was there. After we finished, we went to his bank where he prepared a draft for five thousand ducats. I asked him to make it out to Pierre Luin.

"Why? Who is he?" Mathis inquired.

"My financial manager," I said.

"You have a financial manager?" Mathis exclaimed. "Why, you're just an adventurer!"

"I suppose that's as good as any title to describe what I do," I said with a laugh. "It has a nice ring. 'Professional Adventurer.' Perhaps I should have calling cards made with that."

"Are you making fun of me?" Mathis asked in a testy voice.

"Absolutely not," I replied quickly. "I hope I am laughing *with* you, but certainly not *at* you. I quite like being called an adventurer. It sounds much more noble than thief or swindler."

"I never intended you to believe that I hold that view of you," he protested.

"Well, it is what I do," I confessed, "although I also like to think I am helping people when the law cannot."

"That was certainly the case with me," Mathis said. "By the time the law weighed in, my idiot brother would have pawned everything. Speaking of which, I should warn the housekeeper to take a few days off, perhaps. Vincent is likely to be in bad temper, and I would hate for him to take out his frustration on her."

19

It was several months more before anyone disturbed my peaceful idleness. The summer solstice was ten days away, and the heat of summer was making itself felt. I was on my way to visit my salle when a short, heavyset man came puffing up behind me.

"Excuse me," he gasped. "Are you Casimir FitzDuncan?"

"I am," I replied, turning to face him.

"I was in the book shop when you left," he said. "They pointed you out to me, and, well, you walk rather quickly."

"How can I help you, Mister—?" I asked.

"Williams," he said, still panting. "Brent Williams."

"How can I help you, Mr. Williams?" I inquired again.

"I understand you help people recover things that have been lost or stolen. Is that right?"

"Close enough," I said.

"I need your help," he said. "I want you to get my daughter back."

"Your daughter? Has she been kidnapped?" I asked.

"No, not exactly," Williams said. "Look, it's complicated. Can we sit down somewhere and discuss it?"

My rooms above the book shop were as close as anything else. The nearest inn was the Foaming Boar, but it was further away. The subject seemed personal enough that I guessed Williams would prefer a private setting.

"We'll go back to my rooms above the book shop, if that's acceptable," I offered.

"That's fine," Williams said. "Just—please don't walk so fast. My legs are short and—"

"You set the pace, Mr. Williams," I suggested.

When we returned to my rooms, I gestured toward my sofa. I took the chair facing him. Then I waited for him to begin speaking. It took longer than I expected.

"Sorry," Williams said. "It's a complicated story. I thought I knew where to start, but now I'm not sure that's the right place."

"Begin anywhere you like," I said. "You can unravel the threads later. Where is your daughter?"

"Right. Well, she's not exactly my daughter," Williams said. "She's the daughter of my best friend, John Tilden."

"Why isn't he here?" I asked.

"He's dead," Williams said.

"Oh."

"She might as well be my daughter," Williams explained. "I'm the closest thing to family she has left."

"And where is she?"

"I don't know, exactly," he said. "But I do know who she's with—a man named Hank Allen."

"Did he kidnap her?"

"No. Not exactly," Williams said.

"What does 'not exactly' mean?" I asked.

"She probably went with him at first because she thought she wanted to. I don't think that's the case anymore."

"Why not?"

"One of her friends saw her a few days ago," Williams said. "She said that Tillie—that's her name—"

"Tillie Tilden?" I asked. "Did her parents hate her?"

"Not at all," Williams said. "They named her Matilda. It was only later that they—"

"I understand," I said. "Please continue."

"When her friend saw Tillie, she said it looked as though Tillie had suffered a beating. Before Tillie could talk to her friend, Hank Allen appeared and hustled

Tillie away—rather violently, according to the friend. He snatched her arm roughly and yanked her hard."

"Mr. Williams, if this is a case where she is being mistreated, perhaps the authorities—"

"The authorities can't help," Williams stated firmly. "Well, they could, but I don't want them involved."

"Why not?"

"Ten years ago, Tillie's father and I were partners," Williams explained.

"Partners in what?"

"Burglary," Williams said.

I managed to keep from laughing out loud. Brent Williams—huffing, puffing, overweight—looked nothing like a burglar. He saw my look of incredulity.

"My partner, John Tilden, is the one who did the actual stealing," he said. "I worked as a butler and identified where the important things were hidden."

"How could that work?" I asked. "Surely people would become suspicious if all your employers ended up being robbed."

"I moved around quite a bit," he said, "and changed my name a couple of times. Plus, I had outstanding references."

"No one ever checked your references, did they?" I surmised.

"Not once. Anyway, John approached me when I was working—legitimately—for August Braintree," Williams resumed. "He asked if I enjoyed my position. In our first few meetings, I would not answer and changed the subject. The truth of the matter is that August Braintree is an ass, and his whole family is snotty and unpleasant. I disliked working for them a great deal. Eventually, I admitted that to John. He told me he already knew that, which is why he approached me in the first place. 'How would you like to put one over on them?' he asked me. I made him explain."

"Let me guess," I said. "You would find out where they kept their valuables and tell Tilden. Then, the two of you would figure out the best time to strike. Tilden would sneak in and make the grab. You would be in the clear because you would be with the family when the robbery took place. Later, you would split the proceeds. Is that right?"

"Accurate enough," Williams said. "One thing I should tell you is that we never took the largest and most valuable pieces, and we did not take everything. John felt that doing so would cause too much of an uproar. He would grab a couple of the items of middling value and actually looked for those that seemed like they had not been used much. His idea was that some of our victims would think they misplaced things instead of being robbed. He was correct in a few instances."

"When the owners noticed them missing, they thought they lost them?" I clarified.

"Yes," Williams confirmed. "When I left their employ, I was under no suspicion. A couple of them wrote glowing letters of recommendation for me."

"What did you do with the stolen items?" I asked.

"Not much," Williams said. "The most valuable things were jewels, but Tilden said that trying to sell them immediately would make it easy for the authorities to find us. We took some of the gold settings and hammered them into lumps, then sold the gold to generate some cash to live on. That was mostly for him. John had a wife and daughter, and the money mostly went to them. Our plan with the jewels was to gather enough of them over a couple of years so that we could both retire and live comfortably without needing to work."

"What happened?"

"I thought we reached our goal," Williams said. "John wanted to do one more job. I argued against it. One of the grooms saw him go into the house and caught him in the act. They arrested him, took him to court, and sent him to prison for ten years."

"Is he still there?" I asked.

"No. John died in prison about two months ago," Williams said. "What makes things more complicated is that his wife fell ill and died shortly after John was sent away. Tillie was only twelve. John begged me to take her in and raise her until he finished his sentence."

"How long ago was this?" I asked.

"Almost eight years ago," Williams answered.

"Where are the things the two of you stole?" I asked.

"Hidden," Williams said. "Like before, I've used some of the gold and platinum from the settings to pay expenses but have not touched the jewels."

"Where does this Hank Allen figure in?"

"Allen shared a cell with John," Williams said. "I think what happened is that he learned that John and I had these jewels hidden away, and he killed John. A few weeks later, Allen's sentence was up, and he planned to find out from Tillie where the jewels were."

"And then?" I prompted.

"Hank Allen found where Tillie and I were. When he showed up, he informed us that he shared John's cell and claimed they had become good friends. He tried to tell me that John wanted me to share the jewels with him. I didn't believe him for a second. When he realized that I was not going to fall for his lies, he started to sweet talk Tillie."

"And he was successful?"

"Yes. Tillie's rather plain, and simple-minded on top of that," Williams said. "Having a good-looking man like Hank Allen paying attention to her went to her head, especially since he claimed to be her father's good friend. The two of them disappeared about ten days ago."

"And Allen is trying to find out where the jewels are from Tillie?" I surmised.

"I'm sure he has tried," Williams said. "But Tillie has no idea where they are. She doesn't even know they exist."

"That would explain her battered appearance," I said.

"It would," Williams agreed. "Then yesterday, I received a note from Allen. He told me he would continue to abuse Tillie until I gave him all the jewels. The longer I took, the more she would suffer."

"Do you know where he is?"

"I do not," Williams said. "He told me to meet him at an inn named the Oaken Bucket for dinner this evening at seven o'clock. The inn is in the Kettle."

"What do you think will happen if you do not meet him?" I asked.

"Tillie will get a beating, or worse," Williams said glumly. "I can't let that happen. John entrusted her to me. I'm the nearest thing she has to a father."

"What do you think I can do?" I asked.

"I hope you can get her away from him," Williams said. "The story is that your fee is half of what you recover. I can't place a value on Tillie's head, but I'll give you half of the jewels. I don't know what they're worth, but it's probably a lot."

"How do I reach you, Mr. Williams?" I asked. "I need to think about your situation before I agree to help you."

Williams gave me his address. It was not far from where Callahan and Cheatham used to live. I told him I would be in touch.

He was distressed that I did not agree to help him immediately. There was no way I could promise that. I felt bad for Tillie, but the idea being compensated for helping Williams by sharing in ill-gotten gains went against my grain. There was also the prospect of violence, based how Williams described Hank Allen.

After he departed, I headed for the Palace of Justice. The clerk at the end of the entrance corridor tried to stop me, but I ignored him. I marched up to Sir Oliver's office and sprawled in the chair facing his desk.

"I need your help, Ollie," I said.

"*You* need *my* help, Mr. FitzDuncan?" he asked with his eyebrows raised. "That's not how our relationship works. *I* give *you* orders. You follow them or risk incurring my great displeasure."

"Ollie, I thought we'd moved beyond that," I wheedled. "Haven't I been a good lad these last few months?"

"You have been, which is why you're still able to walk the streets as a free man," he responded.

"Fine. Then as a citizen of Aquileia, I am calling upon the City Watch to render aid," I said.

"Go to the desk downstairs," Sir Oliver grumbled, jerking his thumb over his shoulders.

"Oh, c'mon, Ollie," I pleaded. "It's an interesting story. At least hear me out."

"Go ahead," he sighed. "You've already interrupted me."

Taking a deep breath, I launched into the story. I recounted what Williams told me. When I finished, Sir Oliver looked at me over his steepled fingers.

"Do you want the City Watch involved to make it easier for you to claim half of the loot?" he asked.

"Ollie, I don't want the man's money, or jewels, or whatever," I protested. "It wouldn't feel right. I want to free the girl from this Hank Allen person. From what Williams said, I think there's a chance that things could turn violent. If that's the case, I don't want to be accused of cold-blooded murder."

"So, if we end up arresting this Williams for theft, it won't bother you?" Sir Oliver asked. "Isn't there honor among thieves?"

"Ollie, I'm not a thief. I'm an adventurer," I stated piously.

It took Sir Oliver a couple of minutes to stop laughing. I will admit I joined in as well, laughing my own joke. Why not? It was funny—delivered perfectly.

"The only problem I would have with you arresting Williams is the girl," I said. "From what he told me, she's not very bright. I would worry about her ability to fend for herself if he takes up residence in prison. You might want to return the jewelry to the rightful owners, but after all this time, and with a number of pieces missing their settings, getting the right items back to the respective owners will be a matter of pure guesswork."

"Are you saying I should look the other way regarding Williams and the crimes in which he took part?" Sir Oliver asked.

"I would never try to tell you how to do your job, Ollie," I said. "I take that back—I would never ordinarily tell you how to do your job. If I see you completely cock things up, however, I reserve the right to express my opinion."

"But you think I should—"

"Ollie, if this were an easy problem to resolve, I certainly would not have come to you seeking advice, eh? Let's start with getting the girl away from Hank Allen. After that, I don't have any answers."

"And you want my help because you think a confrontation with this Allen fellow might turn violent?"

"Exactly," I said. "If things turn out poorly, I don't want you thinking I'm off on a murderous rampage. That was the term you used months ago, wasn't it? Murderous rampage?"

"Has anyone ever told you that you can be annoying?" Sir Oliver asked.

"Not since I was a boy," I said. "I imagine the armsmen at Easton Manor would probably agree with your assessment."

"Where and when is Williams supposed to meet Hank Allen?"

"Tonight, seven o'clock, at the Oaken Bucket," I said.

"Seven Hells!" Sir Oliver cursed. "That's in the heart of the Kettle."

"So?"

"We—the City Watch—somewhat leave the residents of the Kettle to their own devices after dark," Sir Oliver said. "There is a fully staffed outpost there, and if there is a fire at night, we will respond. As far as maintaining law and order, though, we only venture out from sunup to sundown."

"In other words, you won't help me," I said.

"The City Watch will not be able to help you," Sir Oliver said. "It would be too dangerous for my men. Their presence would cause a commotion, which, I dare say, would not be beneficial in terms of recovering the young lady."

"I'm on my own, then," I said.

"Not necessarily," he stated.

"You just said the City Watch cannot help me."

"I did."

"Then I'm on my own."

"Perhaps I may accompany you, Caz," Sir Oliver said. "If only to make sure you do not embark on another murderous rampage."

"But you're the Principal of the City Watch," I protested. "You can't—"

"Perhaps tonight I leave the trapping of my office behind and be merely an adventurer," he said and started to laugh.

After agreeing to meet Sir Oliver at the Oaken Bucket at half past six, I left the Palace of Justice. I found a hackney waiting outside, hired him, and drove to where Williams said he lived. After asking the driver to wait, I knocked on the door and told Williams I would help him.

"I'll be at the Oaken Bucket in advance of your meeting with Hank Allen," I said. "Don't acknowledge my presence at all. Don't look at me, don't wave—nothing. When Hank Allen arrives, tell him whatever you need to—make up a reason for delaying. I'll follow him from the inn and find Tillie."

"Thank you, Mr. FitzDuncan," he said, clasping my hand in both of his. "Thank you."

Of course, I did not share with Williams that Sir Oliver would be accompanying me, and that he might very well find himself locked in a cell after tonight. It bothered me slightly. Williams came to me in good faith. On the other hand, he freely confessed to being an accomplice in a number of robberies. I hoped Sir Oliver would consider leniency, as it was Tilden who performed the actual thefts, but if we freed the girl from danger, that would be enough to soothe my conscience.

<h1 style="text-align:center">20</h1>

Not willing to trust the quality of the cuisine at the Oaken Bucket, I took an early dinner at the Foaming Boar. When I finished eating, I returned to my rooms and donned the "working man's clothes" that I purchased for my role as an itinerant groom. I felt those would help me fit in down in the Kettle. My sword was not something a regular fellow would carry, so I left it behind, as well as most of the contents of my purse. I did slide a knife in one boot, and the cosh in the other.

I found a hackney in the market square outside and asked him to take me to a neighborhood next to the Kettle. After he dropped me off, I walked the rest of the way. I had no idea where the Oaken Bucket was, so I needed to ask some passers-by. Hearing my foreign accent—at least, foreign to the Kettle—generated skeptical looks. After they judged me by the clothes I wore, they shared with me where to go.

I found a seat at a small table in the common room of the inn. Not long after I sat down and was served a mug of hard cider, Sir Oliver entered. I breathed a sigh of relief when I saw his attire was similar to mine. Without saying a word, he came over and joined me.

We made small talk—about the weather mostly. We had the same goal. Neither of us wanted to seem as though we were waiting for someone.

"I hope you ate before coming," I said quietly.

"While my people tell me the Oaken Bucket is not the worst food in the Kettle," he said, "they advised me to dine elsewhere. I did not want a rebellious gut to spoil my 'adventure' this evening."

A few minutes before seven, Brent Williams arrived. He scanned the people in the common room. For a moment, I thought he would give me away, but he broke eye contact before it became too obvious. He took a seat at a small table diagonally across from us.

"That's Williams, the fat man sitting alone," I whispered to Sir Oliver as I nodded very slightly in the proper direction.

Sir Oliver did not look until over a minute later. He made it appear as though he was searching for the serving girl. She noticed him and came over.

"Again," was all he said, indicating both our mugs.

After she departed, a thin man marked by the pastiness of his skin entered. He looked around. When he saw Williams, he strolled over and joined him.

I nodded to Sir Oliver. He turned as though looking for the serving girl again. Then he looked back at me.

"That's a prison pallor if ever I've seen one," he whispered. "I take it that's our man?"

"From the looks of it, yes," I said. "He and Williams are having a rather intense discussion. Whatever Williams is telling him is not what he wants to hear."

Our serving girl returned. I paid her quickly, as I feared the discussion between Williams and Allen looked like it might end any moment. While I could not make out exactly what Allen was saying, I could hear his tone. It was cold and menacing.

"Drink up," I said to Sir Oliver a minute later. "Our boy is leaving."

"At least the cider here is good," Sir Oliver said as he stood, wiping his lips.

"I don't think they would dare try to cheat their customers on their drinks," I remarked. "They'd burn the place down if they did."

We walked past Williams. He looked as though he wanted to stand and talk, but I made a small gesture to keep him in his seat. Sir Oliver and I walked out of the inn. Hank Allen was walking away to the right. We let him get a couple of blocks away before we started following.

"Make it look as though we are having a conversation," Sir Oliver advised. "In case he looks back."

"Fine," I replied. "You mentioned 'prison pallor' to describe Allen."

"You only get that particular paleness of skin by spending years away from the sun—in prison," Sir Oliver said. "And quite a few criminals fall back into their old ways before they lose it. It makes it easy for my men to spot them."

Allen then stopped and turned around. Sir Oliver and I kept walking at our unhurried pace. Since Allen was looking for Brent Williams, he did not register us as a threat. He turned left at the next corner.

"If he looks back and sees us again," Sit Oliver said, "we will need to split up. I'll tell you what to do if that happens."

Fortunately, Allen did not turn around again. We continued to follow him from roughly two blocks behind. Allen reached a doorway, opened the door and went inside.

Sir Oliver and I reached the door. He stepped aside and indicated I should open it. I tried to defer to him but he shook his head.

Perhaps it's a good thing he didn't. Allen was waiting for us. As soon as I opened the door, he lunged forward, trying to stab me with a knife.

My reactions were quick enough that his blow was not lethal. He did stab me in my left side. Before Allen recovered his balance, Sir Oliver punched him in the left side of his head, staggering him. I slugged him from the right, and Allen went down.

"Take this," I said, pulling the cosh out of my boot and offering it to Sir Oliver. "In case he needs to go to sleep again. I'm going to look for the girl."

"I have my own," Sir Oliver said, twirling a similar leather cosh by a strap around his fingers. "The girl probably isn't in this building. He was onto us. We'll need for him to wake up to tell us where to go."

"I'm going to look anyway," I said.

There were four doors on the ground floor. Each one opened onto a single room. All them held tenants who glared at me when I burst through the door. A few noticed the spreading bloodstain on my shirt. I could tell by the way their eyes widened.

Heading up the stairs, there were four more doors. Tillie was behind none of them. I trudged back down to where Sir Oliver waited, standing over the unconscious form of Hank Allen. With the adrenalin leaving my system, my side was starting to hurt.

"No luck," I said.

"Well, we need to get him out here before any of the people you just bothered come out to see what is happening," Sir Oliver said. "We're about five blocks from the outpost. Let's carry him there."

Sir Oliver lifted Allen up by his armpits. He gave me the lighter end—the feet—because he saw how the blood was spreading on my shirt. After a couple of blocks, he told me to stop and rest. I was only too happy to do so. My strength was fading.

Sir Oliver surprised me by hoisting Allen up over his shoulder and continuing on. When I tried to protest, he waved me off. I wasn't terribly eager to try carrying Allen again, so I kept quiet.

Sir Oliver carried the limp form all the way to the City Watch building. He described it as an outpost. "Fortress" might have been a better word.

In the ramshackle construction that characterized the Kettle, the City Watch building was sturdy and squat. It was built using thick brownstone blocks. A hurricane could blow through (which actually happened generally once a decade) and not damage it at all.

When we arrived, Sir Oliver kicked the door and hollered. A small grate at eye level opened. Seeing Sir Oliver, the man's eyes went wide. He opened the door quickly. Sir Oliver dropped Allen's body to the floor once he was inside.

"This one," he pointed at Allen, "in a cell. Get us some bandages. Caz—sit yourself down before you collapse."

I slumped onto the bench just inside the entrance. Two men appeared and dragged Allen away. A man hurried up carrying bandages.

"You have any training?" Sir Oliver asked.

"Some," the man answered.

"That's more than I do. Get to work."

The man knelt down beside me. He lifted my shirt and whistled inwardly when he saw my wound. He seemed to freeze for a moment.

"I need to clean the blood away," he explained as he stood. "Then I'll wrap you up."

He scurried away. A minute later, he reappeared with a bowl and a washcloth. He began wiping the blood away from where I was stabbed.

"Cheer up, Caz," Sir Oliver said. "It could have been me."

"Ha, ha," I said sourly.

The man tending to me put a pad of gauze over the wound. He then began wrapping more gauze around my middle to hold it in place. When he finished, it was tight but not uncomfortably so.

"That's as good as I know how to do," he said as he stood

"He's awake," came a voice from where they dragged Allen away.

"Uh, Sir Oliver," I said, "this might be something you might want to leave to me."

"Why? Are you planning on torturing the man to get him to tell us where the girl is?" he asked.

"If I need to," I said.

"If it comes to that, I'll make myself scarce," he said. "I think I can convince him to tell us without resorting to damaging him physically."

"Time is probably not our friend," I said. "Who knows what sort of condition he left her in?"

"I'm aware, Caz," he said as he proceeded to the rear of the building.

The rear of the building contained six small cells. There were no windows, and the area smelled of mold and mildew. On either side, there were three cells, separated from one another and fronted with thick iron bars. Sitting on a bunk in the first one was Hank Allen, wearing a smirk.

Sir Oliver found a stool and dragged it over with his foot. He sat down about five yards away from Allen. For at least five minutes, he said nothing.

"Ain't ya gonna ax me some questions?" Allen sneered.

"Wasn't planning on it," Sir Oliver said calmly.

"Dontcha wanna know where the girl is?"

"Makes my job simpler if she dies," Sir Oliver said in a bored tone, examining his fingernails. "She dies, you hang. You should have been hanged when we sent you away last time. I don't know why the magistrate didn't call for it then. I'm going to need to look and see if he's that soft all the time."

"Cuz I din't deserve no hangin' that's why," Allen said.

"Sure you did," Sir Oliver continued, still acting bored. "You beat a man to death. Magistrate should have strung you up."

"He weren't dead when I was arrested," Allen said with smugly.

"No, he stuck around for a few days," Sir Oliver said, still bored. "The beating you gave him is what killed him, though. Blood clot in the brain. You'll be happy to know he never woke up after you were finished with him, so he only suffered while you were pulping him. Anyway, if the girl dies, you hang. So, I don't want to know where she is. Let's go home, Caz."

Sir Oliver stood and slid the stool back to the corner. He gestured for me to go through the door first. As I did, Allen squawked.

"You ain't gonna ax me nothin'?"

"No. Goodbye, Mr. Allen. See you on the scaffold," Sir Oliver said as he left.

"Wait!"

"What do you want?" Sir Oliver said in an annoyed tone.

"She's at my place. Number six at 53 Elwood Street. You'll find her there."

Sir Oliver said nothing. We continued out. When we reached his men, we stopped.

"We need a couple of you to take us to that address," Sir Oliver said.

Two of the men volunteered. We left the building. It took us about ten minutes to reach the address.

Number six was upstairs. I followed Sir Oliver upstairs. We went through the door and saw the poor girl tied to the chair, a gag in her mouth. Her face was bruised—both eyes blackened. When she saw us, she started to cry.

Sir Oliver quickly cut her bonds and removed the gag. She tried to stand, but her feet must have been asleep from being bound. Sir Oliver caught her before she fell. Tillie clung to him, sobbing.

"Check her wounds, Caz," Sir Oliver asked. "Can she travel?"

Her wrists and ankles were rubbed raw. Looking at her face made me wince. She was homely to begin with—the beatings Allen gave her did not improve her looks. I imagined the bruises under her clothes were just as deep and as extensive. She smelled of urine.

"It might be better if she spent the night at the outpost," I said. "I don't think she will be able to make it on foot."

"Tillie, we're going to take you to the City Watch's building nearby," Sir Oliver said. "We'll let you rest overnight and feed you. How long has it been since you ate?"

Tillie cried and babbled. Neither of us could make sense of what she was saying. I thought I heard her say "a couple of days" somewhere in there, but I couldn't be sure.

We made it to the City Watch outpost and ushered her inside. Sir Oliver ordered the men to fetch water and whatever remained of their evening meal. There wasn't much—half of a loaf of bread. Tillie seized it and immediately began gnawing on it. Every so often, she stopped and gulped down some water.

"Make sure she rests easy, men," Sir Oliver said. "Someone will come to collect her tomorrow. One of you give up your bunk for her. And by all the heavenly beings, don't let her see or hear the prisoner!"

"Aye, Sir Oliver," the one who seemed to be in charge said.

"Tillie, we're leaving now," I said, kneeling down to her level. "We'll send Mr. Williams to come get you in the morning. These nice men will take care of you tonight. Do you understand?"

She nodded vigorously. I stood and caught Sir Oliver's eye. He started to head for the door.

"I think I like being an 'adventurer.' Granted, I always expected the damsels I would rescue would be beautiful, but for a first time, I'll take it," he said.

"This is my first damsel as well," I said. "I do hope they get prettier."

"Plenty of room for improvement, then," Sir Oliver cracked.

"Let's hope," I said. "Um, not to bring up a sore subject, but have you decided what you will do about Brent Williams?"

"Are you planning on demanding your usual terms?" Sir Oliver asked.

"I already told you that I would not," I said. "In my other 'adventures,' I helped people regain what was rightfully theirs because it was stolen or they were cheated. They gave me half the value because I made a problem worse than the monetary loss disappear or because I restored some semblance of fairness. I don't want a share of stolen loot. That doesn't sit well with me."

"But we did restore some fairness to the world," Sir Oliver said. "Tillie will return to Mr. Williams, who I presume was serious when he told you he would care for her—and she will need a lifetime of care, from what I saw."

"I agree. From your remark, should I gather that you do not intend to pursue Mr. Williams on criminal charges, Ollie?" I asked.

"It actually depended entirely on you, Caz," he said. "If you told me that you intended to demand your usual fee, that would have irritated me, and I would then have Mr. Williams arrested and taken away anything he gave you. Instead, you showed me that something else motivates you. It's not the money, is it?"

"To be perfectly frank, Ollie, I never thought about it much until this came up," I said. "I was mostly doing it to help people. The money was nice—I cannot lie—but I would have helped Freddy for nothing, and that's what started this."

"You really did not intend to kill Callahan and Cheatham, did you?" Sir Oliver asked.

"I did not. You see that now, don't you?"

"In my position, I see the most accomplished liars, Caz," Sir Oliver said. "And if I generally start off thinking the worst of people, I'm rarely disappointed. I'm not going to apologize for misjudging you—you did kill two men who, while criminals, did not deserve to die. You said it was in self-defense, and I now find that completely believable."

"Does this mean my period of being on parole is finished?" I asked.

"Absolutely not!" Sir Oliver said with a grin. "You still have months to go before the year is up. And even after that, you know if I call on you, I will not take your refusing my summons at all well."

ABOUT THE AUTHOR

John Spearman has been a Fortune 500 sales and marketing executive, a Latin teacher and coach at a prestigious New England boarding school, and is now an author. He lives in coastal Maine with his wife and their dogs. He began writing because his wife challenged him. He was lucky enough to find an audience and has not looked back (except to fix the mistakes he made in the early days!).

This book is the tenth of the FitzDuncan series, and serves as a prequel to the first book, *FitzDuncan.*

Spearman has four other book series, all in the category of military science fiction. The first was the Jonah Halberd series of four books. The Sandy Pike series (also four books) is set in a different universe from the Halberd books. The next series is of three novels, featuring a female hero named Perseverance Andrews These are related to the Jonah Halberd series. The Andrews books take place in the same universe, though over three hundred years earlier. Mercenary Navy is the title of the most recent series, published by AethonBooks. It consists (so far) of three books: *Rawlins's Redemption, Swiftsure Ascendant,* and *Tenuous Defense.*

If you enjoyed reading this book, please consider leaving a positive review on amazon.com or goodreads.com. It will help other readers like you find books they might enjoy. To learn more about the author's different works, please visit www.johnjspearmanauthor.com